A CANDLELIGHT INTRIGUE

This Book Provided by
Project: LEARN (Books For People)
Interchurch Council
664-1691

NOT FOR RESALE

CANDLELIGHT ROMANCES

504 CAMERON'S LANDING, *Anne Stuart*
506 THE WIDOW'S ESCORT, *Beth de Bilio*
508 THE WEB OF DECEPTION, *Francesca Chimenti*
510 PEREGRINE HOUSE, *Janis Flores*
514 THE PHANTOM REFLECTION, *Ann Ashton*
518 THE HAUNTING OF SARA LESSINGHAM, *Margaret James*
519 SEARCH FOR YESTERDAY, *Barbara Doyle*
520 PERILOUS HOMECOMING, *Genevieve Slear*
522 STOLEN DREAMS, *Stephanie Kincaid*
523 DEMONWOOD, *Anne Stuart*
524 TEARS IN PARADISE, *Jane Blackmore*
525 LOVE'S SWEET ILLUSION, *Suzanne Roberts*
526 DESTINY IN ROME, *Frances Carfi Matranga*
528 THE COACHMAN'S DAUGHTER, *Donna Creekmore*
529 IMAGE OF EVIL, *Rosemary A. Crawford*
531 FIRST A DREAM, *Marie Pershing*
532 PASSIONATE SUMMER, *Belle Thorne*
533 VILLE-MARIE, *Bernice Wolf*
534 THE GHOST OF LUDLOW FAIR, *Evelyne Hayworth*
535 LOVE IS LIKE THAT, *Irene Lawrence*
536 EMBERS OF THE HEART, *Candice Arkham*
538 DRAGONSEED, *Barbara Banks*
539 GRAVETIDE, *Carolyn McKnight*
540 THE LONG ENCHANTMENT, *Helen Nuelle*
541 SECRET LONGINGS, *Nancy Kennedy*
544 GUARDIAN OF INNOCENCE, *Judy Boynton*
545 RING THE BELL SOFTLY, *Margaret James*
546 LEGACY OF THE HEART, *Lorena McCourtney*
547 FAREWELL TO ALEXANDRIA, *Suzanne Roberts*
550 HOME TO THE HIGHLANDS, *Jessica Eliot*
551 DARK LEGACY, *Candace Connell*
552 OMEN FOR LOVE, *Ester Boyd*
553 MAYBE TOMORROW, *Marie Pershing*
556 WHERE SHADOWS LINGER, *Janis Susan May*
557 THE DEMON COUNT, *Anne Stuart*
558 NO TIME FOR LOVE, *Lori Herter*
559 THE MIDNIGHT EMBRACE, *Barbara Doyle*
560 RUTHANA, *Margaret Nettles Ogan*
561 THE DEMON COUNT'S DAUGHTER, *Anne Stuart*

THE PEACOCK BED

Joanne Marshall

A CANDLELIGHT INTRIGUE

*For Mona and Jos,
much love*

Published by
Dell Publishing Co., Inc.
1 Dag Hammarskjold Plaza
New York, New York 10017

Copyright © 1978 by Joanne Marshall

All rights reserved. For information address St. Martin's
Press, Inc., New York, New York.

Dell ® TM 681510, Dell Publishing Co., Inc.

ISBN: 0-440-16883-X

Reprinted by arrangement with St. Martin's Press, Inc.

Printed in the United States of America

First Dell printing—May 1980

THE
PEACOCK
BED

ONE

The carriage rattled and swayed as it took a wide bend descending sharply through a green mesh of branches that allowed fugitive gleams from the river. Abigail drew a deep, satisfied breath as her stomach subsided quite pleasurably, leaving her with an inclination to burst out laughing. The banks of the Tweed were quite beautiful; in fact, the whole Border scene had exceeded expectations. Any indecision she had experienced initially had long since dissipated under the magic of round fairy hills and wild valleys where there was nothing but the occasional sheep or the stone ring of a fold, the crumbled tower of a peel.

Not for the first time she wondered why Charity Scott had invited her for a prolonged stay. They had got on well enough at finishing school and Charity had been kind when her parents had died in the epidemic, yet there had not been the closeness one might have imagined essential for a lengthy visit. If she had not felt so bereft, so motiveless, she might have refused. As it was, she was charmed beyond measure by the slowly unfolding pageantry of the so-called Bloody Border, seeing not the ghosts of yesterday but the bouncing foliage, the secret stone cottages, the decayed fortresses that were now anachronisms. There would be none of the old feuding spirit nowadays, not in 1862. The ruins were interesting, but at an immense distance like the Roman occupation or the depredations of Henry VIII in his anger against anything Scots. He'd had a bonny rampage over the Border, burning and destroying as Cromwell had done much later. The Abbeys had suffered most, being hollow shells that somehow managed to retain a total dignity in spite of their rooflessness, the open gaps of their tall windows, the encroaching weeds. The Rough Wooing, they called Henry's period of destruction. It sounded exciting, Abigail thought, smoothing her tumbled skirts after the hectic tussle at the last curve of the road, her cheeks flushing, eyes bright. Any tentative romances she had so far experienced had been tepid affairs, stupid and abortive. A rough wooing sounded the perfect antidote and Borderers were still the same stock as those who reived and raided two or three centuries ago. Surely all the fire and passion had not been entirely subjugated? She'd not believe it. How much better to be snatched to the pommel of a saddle and carried off in the arms of a lover than the anaemic encounters that were all she previously knew of the opposite sex.

She pushed her head out of the window, sniffing at the fragrant air, and was startled by the sight of what appeared to be a sinister bundle of rags. But the bundle moved and scrambled up. The horses reared, showing steep black backs and disordered manes, dragging themselves to a standstill. A gipsy stood there, dark eyes glittering, walnut-creased skin shining with sweat. A basket filled with newly-whittled pegs stood by her side.

'Ah, my fine, fiery lady,' she crooned, hand outstretched, 'cross my palm with silver and I'll tell you your fortune. That pretty, red hair will reach a target. Those bonny green eyes will smite like an arrow.

There's luck around you, my sonsy miss. A house ahead of you with pink in its stones – '

Pink? Abigail wondered. She'd imagined Duncraw to be black and brown or a sooty grey. Yet this old harridan had obviously just left its back door and knew it to be rose-coloured. She could not believe a word the woman uttered. But a spark of admiration was kindled by the effrontery of the approach and she did have a coin to spare for one less fortunate.

'Very well,' she said loudly for the benefit of the coachman. 'You may tell my fortune if you are not too long about it,' and fished around in her reticule for a piece of silver.

The brown, callused fist closed over it greedily. The coin disappeared into the maw of a frayed pocket, then her own hand was taken between leathery palms, surprisingly gentle. A thick finger traced the delicate lines. 'I see – I see a man in grey – on a horse.'

'Is that good?' Abigail demanded, shaking away a strand of red hair that obscured her left eye, aware of the note of reserve in the gipsy's voice.

'There are shadows,' the woman replied after a pause. 'Shadows – '

'Is there nothing more substantial?' Abigail asked, disappointed, noting the restlessness of the horses. 'I should have thought my silver would have bought more – '

'You'd not have me tell you lies?'

'No – '

'There is more. I see – death.'

'Death?' The green branches swept downwards in a spiteful gust of wind. The woman shivered and nodded.

'Aye. Death. Water – '

'Drowning?'

'No. Something else.' The black eyes stared at her

starkly. 'But it's not all dark. There's something you've looked for and never found.'

'And what name would you put to it?' Abigail questioned softly. 'What?'

'The shadows are over it – like a cloaked man –'

'A grey cloak?'

'It's not clear enough. I see only a shape –'

'No – happiness?' Abigail felt cheated.

'If there is, it must struggle free.'

'Nothing more?' The red hair had blown back, tickling her cheek.

'No more.'

'Very well. I respect you for avoiding untruths just to satisfy me. I hoped, as women always do, for a shaft of hope –'

'It could be there –'

'But behind the shadows.'

'That's right, young miss. But I do see birds.' The voice became animated. 'Birds –'

'There are birds everywhere.'

'Not like these. Royal birds.'

'Indeed?' Abigail subsided on to the buttoned seat. Royal birds. She could think of nothing but phoenixes or rocs and they lived only in legends. The road twisted and the woman was left behind in her own secret world.

They followed the course of a stream that ran out of the Tweed. It chattered over a stony bed, its soft conversational sound mingling with the wind, the muted bird-song, the carriage's rattle and jingle. Grey, the wind whispered, and the birds that flew from a thicket were the same sad colour.

Abigail tried to picture Charity. It was some time since she had seen her. There had been the distressing time of her own parents' deaths and the period of readjustment. She had been left a small income, adequate for quiet living but no inducement for fortune-hunters. She was glad. If there was never a man who would want her for herself, that was better than to buy a relationship based on falsehood.

The tough moorland turned to a walled estate set with trees, behind which the hill sloped like the back of a fish. A gatehouse came into view, small, with a steeply-pitched roof and stepped gable. The stonework was a pale, dusky pink and clustered about with laurel and holly. A dark, frowning man waited by the door, broad-shouldered and tough-looking, his hands backed with a fuzz of black hair. His animal-like aura was intimidating. Even his voice when he spoke was heavy and growling. He opened the gates reluctantly to allow the carriage to drive inside, then threw them back so that the heavy metal shuddered against its hinges. Like a prison door, Abigail thought, then grimaced at her own fancy.

The carriage was swallowed up by two high ramparts of shrubs backed by trees. Crows nested in a clump of elms which had probably been there as long as the house, for craw was the Scots name for the birds. Royal? Abigail shook her head. Black and ragged, they were more scarecrow than noble.

The trees petered out to reveal stretches of grass and winding paths that led to the long, shallow incline of the hill. And then, with a shock of delight, the house came into view, long and gracious, with large windows and a steeple at the back, a huge porch that shadowed the main door. There were yew trees, great dark blots against the lighter colours of field and foliage, the greyish pink of the façade. The house, the hill and the gardens fused into a perfect whole. Strange that Charity had often seemed dissatisfied. This place should have been a joy. Of course her mother had been dead for years. Such an early bereavement could colour a child's life, particularly if the death had been sudden or violent. The light seemed to go out of the sky, leaving the scene like dull tints on a tapestry.

Abigail noticed something she had missed previously. Halfway up the hill was a small enclosure containing a tiny chapel. A few gravestones protruded beyond the low wall. The Scotts must be an important family if they had their own burial-ground. Charity's mother would lie there.

The door was flung open just before the carriage reached the forecourt and Charity ran out on to the wide step, her yellow curls bobbing, her pale face wreathed in smiles of welcome. A manservant followed, as dark and taciturn-looking as the gatehouse-keeper and with the now recognizable thin lips and suggestion of hirsuteness. He stared at Abigail in the same unfriendly fashion, negating Charity's kindlier reception. Stolidly he went to remove her trunk, assisted by the coachman, who also had astonishingly hairy hands. It was not impossible that they were all members of the same family. There was a strange, nightmare quality in the thought of being attended by a race of shaggy bondsmen. Of course, the Lowlands had their own clan system, as had the Highlanders, and family characteristics in the enclosed life of sept and country must be more noticeable than in the freer sphere of city liaisons.

'You must be worn out,' Charity said, tossing her golden hair in a well-remembered gesture. Abigail had not really forgotten as much as she imagined. Now that she had set eyes again on the fair Miss Scott, the memories came flooding back. But there was a look she did not recognize, a trace of self-assurance Charity previously lacked. Something had happened to change her. Yet the new perception contained an element of wariness that aroused Abigail's curiosity. She felt warmed and intrigued.

'I am,' she admitted, 'quite weary.'

'Come into the drawing-room. There's no one there. You can relax for a while before you go to change. Take the box upstairs to the Green Room, Ewan.'

'Green?'

'What other colour for you? With those eyes – '

'I am trying to imagine how you cope with red or purple rooms!'

'When eyes give out there are always cheeks and noses.' She giggled.

Charity pushed open a door and a smell of burning logs assailed the air most invitingly. Abigail was aware of a blur of whiteness streaked and blotched with patches of geranium red, of leaping firelight, of rectangles of dark colour framed in shining gilt. 'Oh, how pretty it all is. The white walls are so right with the scarlet, the oak bureau and those paintings. Some parlours are so fussy, all antimacassars and whatnots – '

'Ugh! I know what you mean.'

'And those flowers. Are they from your own gardens?'

'Every one.'

'I saw sheep and cattle. You must be self-sufficient. I dare say there's a well at the back?'

'Of course. And a stream through the grounds. Very necessary in the bad old days.'

'Bad old days?'

'Reiving. Plundering – '

'Oh, yes. I was thinking of that earlier but they seemed more tales than reality.'

'They were certainly not mere tales,' Charity said, collapsing a little inelegantly into a white-covered chair and swinging one foot absent-mindedly. 'Old deeds cast long shadows. You would be surprised how long.' That edge of bitterness was as new as the self-possession. 'But I do not wish to cast a cloud over your arrival. It's good to see you.'

'And you.'

'You'd never believe, would you, that there are still people I am ordered not to know, still whole families reviled by the Pringles – '

'Pringles?' It was pleasant to sit without rattles and jolting, only the crackle of sparks to beat against the eardrums.

'The servants. Apart from the housekeeper they are all Pringles. They only tolerate Mrs Davison because she's related very distantly to one branch of the family.'

'How did Mrs Davison creep into the charmed circle?' Abigail was amused.

'There was a dearth of girl-children for a time and a few deaths of older women who might have qualified for the post. But I'm certain there was a muster of Pringles from Land's End to John o' Groats – secret conclaves – short straws – '

Abigail burst out laughing. 'How delicious! I cannot imagine how I shall keep a straight face when I see the lady.'

'I'm glad you have not lost your sense of humour, Abby. I did wonder – '

Abigail sat up. 'I did for a time. There were only we three and my parents were dear to me. The typhoid is a terrible thing.'

'As the Queen found out to her cost. You would think a prince would be safe. Is it true Victoria is still in the deepest mourning? Hardly ever seen abroad?'

'Quite true. Theirs would seem to be a real love story. A pity she seeks to lay the blame for Albert's death at Edward's door. I think his father's strictness to be the cause of the son's dissolute way of life. A prison cannot make for open behaviour.'

'No,' Charity said, her voice flat. 'How true.'

'But,' Abigail told her decisively, 'I'm over it now. I miss them but I cannot bring them back. I'm not the first to lose mother and father. You yourself – '

'Yes. It was a dreadful shock when my mother had her accident. Hope still does not quite believe she is really gone – '

'That's your young sister?'

'You have a good memory. I think I only spoke to you once of Hope.'

'How old is she now?'

'Seventeen.'

'She did not go away to school?'

'No.' Charity's chin came up. 'She – she had a delicacy and Father thought it better she stayed here with a governess.'

'I should have thought – your company – But it's no business of mine,' Abigail said hurriedly. 'Anyway, if you had not gone away we should never have met and I'd not be sitting here in this dainty withdrawing-room, my nostrils tempted by smells of apple-logs and flowers. It's too peaceful to conjure up pictures of past forays and lingering feuds – '

'They do exist,' Charity said sharply. 'Even in the confines of one's own household.'

Abigail began to feel uncomfortable. 'Perhaps I should change, and a wash would be marvelous. I can trust to my land legs again. Riding in a carriage can be like being aboard ship.'

'I'll show you to your bed-chamber.'

'Shouldn't you pull a bell-rope and summon one of *them*?'

'One of the Pringles? Oh, you are funny, Abby. It will be nice to have you here. You will not go rushing off? Whatever happens?'

'Why should I?'

15

Charity shrugged. 'As you say, why should you. Come, then.'

She led the way up a turning stair and along what once had been a minstrel gallery, broad and comfortable, hung with paintings of men and women almost invariably golden-haired. Abigail was struck by the contrast between Scotts and Pringles. It seemed odd they should have lived cheek by jowl over the centuries, the golden-haired masters, the retainers almost apelike in their ugliness.

The Green Room was decorated with hand-painted Chinese paper, startlingly beautiful, like being in a shadowy garden where birds perched on branches laden with fruit-blossom. A chandelier hung with crystals, chairs seated with deep pink, a small desk by the window, an inlaid press with a row of drawers down one side.

'I had no idea,' Abigail said, impressed, 'that the house would be like this. So grand.'

'What did you expect? A ruined peel?'

'No. Something in between.'

'Aunt Faith would enjoy hearing your opinion. Sometimes I feel she considers it is all hers. She'll die a thousand deaths wondering if you'll bleed against the wallpaper, or drop a vase.'

'I'm not likely to bleed against the plum-blossom, am I? And who is Aunt Faith?'

'Father's sister. She was widowed around the time that Mother died, and left in straitened circumstances. So she and Geoffrey came to live at Duncraw.'

Again, Abigail wondered why, especially with a woman in the house, Charity had not been educated at home with her sister. 'Geoffrey? A cousin?'

'Yes.' Charity seemed inclined to be uncommunicative on the subject of Geoffrey so Abigail refrained from pursuing the topic. She would meet all the persons in the house at the evening meal and could form her own opinions.

'I like that,' Abigail said, pointing to a tall vase filled with dried grasses and peacock feathers.

'Hope did that. She can be quite artistic.'

'I've just realized. Faith, Hope and Charity.'

'I think it's silly. Father had twin sisters who died in infancy. I'm not really fond of most Biblical names. Only Ruth and Rebecca. Although Judith, Salome and Jezebel are attractive. Ours are – dull.' She shrugged expressively.

'Imagine the feelings of a Border minister asked to baptize you Jezebel or Salome!'

'I suppose it would be expecting too much.'

'How could he have overlooked John the Baptist's head, or Jezebel eaten by wild dogs?'

'Was she? I don't care for the Bible. Father enjoys preaching now and again. He used to read passages to his troops. Hod says they called him Gideon. Righteous but a good soldier. A rule-book martinet, he means. Father's is a hell-fire religion.'

'Charity! Hod, who is he?'

'Father's personal body-servant. Like Richard and Blondell. They left the army together.'

'Hod Pringle, I presume?'

'Naturally. Do you imagine they'd allow Father to go off and be attended by just anyone? He might have fallen into the hands of a Young.'

'I'll refrain from asking who the Youngs are, for the present, at least. I have enough to cope with already. I knew the house would be pink, by the way.' Abigail had divested herself of her cape and bonnet and shook free her splendid hair.

'How? I did not tell you.'

'A gipsy accosted me, demanding silver.'

Charity frowned. 'You sent her on her way, I hope?'

'Not immediately. We don't see gipsies in civilized society.'

'Is that an oblique way of saying we are barbarians?'

'No. This house would deny the accusation. But they are peculiar to certain parts of the country or to circuses. I allowed her to look at my palm.'

'What did she say?'

Quite unaccountably, Abigail felt as disinclined to discuss the man in grey and the threat of shadows as Charity had been to speak of her cousin. 'Oh, the usual nothings. I should love that hot water you promised.'

'I completely forgot.' Charity leapt for the bell-pull – a jade green with a gold tassel – and tugged it vigorously. 'Any time you want anything just use this –'

'And be confronted by a Pringle?' Abigail demanded mischievously.

Charity laughed and the traces of discontent and spleen vanished. 'I knew you would bring something refreshing into the place.' For a moment she looked like the child she was when they first met, shy and vulnerable. Someone had hurt her since they parted, Abigail decided with a resurgence of the protective feelings formerly aroused by her friend.

'How long before supper?'

'An hour. I'll leave you to get on. Lie on the bed and close your eyes. I'll come back for you.' Charity was gone before Abigail could demur.

It was quiet after the maid, dark with more than a trace of a moustache, and sullen eyes, came with the copper jug and poured hot water into a flowered china bowl and left green towels on the rail. The journey, part taken by train, had been tiring, and once washed and combed, changed into a gown in readiness for the approaching meal, Abigail was glad to stretch out on the counterpane, her eyes closed.

She became aware, through a fog of drowsiness, of

voices nearby. Now fully awake, she lifted her head, listening intently but unable to make out anything that was said. Something in the studied lowness of the unemotional tones aroused a sensation of unease. Impossible to determine whether they were male or female, but at least she could decide that they came from a room to the left of her own. Her mind whirled with the introduction of all the new names she had heard. Faith, Geoffrey, Hope, a dynasty of black Pringles, the mysterious Youngs and Sir Humphrey Scott, the rule-book martinet. The gipsy, the man in grey, Salome and Jezebel –

The voices stopped. There was a creaking and rustling, then silence. A board squeaked in the passageway. The door began to open very slowly.

'Abigail?' The soft whisper was disturbing – sexless.

Charity peered round the jamb, a soft white shawl around her shoulders. 'I thought you might be asleep.'

Abigail sat up. 'I was. Something woke me. People talking in the next room. The one to the left.'

'That room? You imagined it, my pet. It's not occupied and always locked.'

'I know I heard them.'

'Come and see. We do have a few minutes.'

Abigail followed. Charity turned the handle of the left-hand door but it remained closed for all her pushing.

'How strange,' Abigail murmured.

'I'll get the key and show you later. It's the showpiece of Duncraw.'

The sound of a gong resounded up staircase and hall. They descended in a thoughtful silence.

The most arresting figure at the dining-table was Sir Humphrey. He stood up as Abigail entered, resplendent in black velvet smoking-jacket, blond hair mixed with grey, face magnificently moulded into hollows and protuberances, head slanted in welcome. His eyes were inclined to coolness but that may have had something to do with their sharp blueness. His handclasp was hard and left Abigail's hand tingling.

'We are pleased to see you at Duncraw, Miss Menory.' His voice, too, was harsh, yet not unpleasant.

'And I am equally glad to be here. It's – quite an experience.'

They looked at one another, liking and respecting what they saw. Charity's words came back traitorously. 'His men call him Gideon. A rule-book martinet . . .' Surely she was too hard on him? An officer must be firm and uncompromising. The nature of his calling obliged him to be a leader, to be obeyed without question. It seemed a compliment that he was nicknamed after the outstanding soldier of Biblical times. Abigail wondered which passages he had read to his waiting troops. She had a conviction they had listened.

'Has Charity shown you over the house?'

'Not yet.'

'There's a fair amount to see. You must explore tomorrow.' Her host bowed, his duty done.

They were all seated and, the initial shock of Sir Humphrey's vitality abated, Abigail was free to survey the remaining members of the family. The dark young man who had just subsided into his chair must be Geoffrey. Good-looking up to a certain point but a weak mouth. That grey-haired woman with the doll-like face was probably Faith, sister of Humphrey and the dead twins, Hope and Charity. Hope. Abigail encountered dark, sulky eyes and a fall of brown hair, a reserved expression. Slim, brown hands fiddled with a linen table-napkin. The brown gaze fell away, fixed itself on a flower arrangement in the centre of the cloth. Charity's sister was shy and withdrawn. There may not be time to gain her confidence and know her. It seemed a pity.

Around the room the Pringles stood in watchful attitudes. One had only to replace the livery and uniform to see them still as moss-troopers, in steel bonnets and leather jackets, carrying pikes and axes in place of trays.

Shocked by her own thoughts, for she was not warlike, Abigail sought to subdue her imaginings by engaging in conversation with her neighbour, Charity's cousin Geoffrey. He was disappointingly brusque, his attention returning time and time again to Charity who was always occupied elsewhere. Realization dawned. Geoffrey pursued his cousin and she did not welcome his advances. The tight-lipped attentions of Aunt Faith bore out the truth of Abigail's new-found knowledge. She watched her son and niece with unswerving diligence, blue eyes hard as marbles, the prettiness of her face turned, Medusa-like, to a kind of stone.

No one was dressed in grey.

Abigail drank wine, listened, and felt herself drawn irrevocably towards a Scotland that, once tasted, she was loath to relinquish. It was like nothing she had ever known. The golden Scotts became almost god-like with their attendant hosts of Pringles to care for and nurture them. Yet, through the romantic haze a warning voice whispered, 'Be careful. This is the best of them. There's another side to everything. And everybody...'

'You must see to it, Faith, that there's a special supper tomorrow,' Sir Humphrey was saying, his face wine-flushed, still coldly handsome.

'You – have guests?' Faith, distracted from her scrutiny of Charity and Geoffrey, frowned.

'My dear, must you make it so plain you disapprove?

May I not invite whom I wish to my own house?' His voice was uncharacteristically gentle, almost amused.

The mild reproof brought the colour to his sister's face. 'I did not say I disapproved. I should have thought you might have mentioned it sooner. There's little time to send for fresh provisions. You know how isolated we are.'

'Mrs Rutherford will be dining here and bringing her son.' The hard blue eyes challenged Faith's. The doll-like face paled. 'They will stay on for a few days.'

'Mrs Rutherford?'

'Yes. Is there any reason why she should not come?' he enquired with studious moderation.

Conversation had ceased as the duel progressed. Was it imagination or did Sir Humphrey gain a secret pleasure in baiting his sister? Abigail was certain of it. As though everyone else was the enemy and he reduced to military tactics to win his peacetime wars.

'Why, no.' Even Faith's neck was red. 'I had not realized there was a son – '

'You knew she was a widow. Most widows have children. What is there so unusual in the fact that there is a son of her previous marriage?'

'You said nothing – '

'Must I tell you everything?' The gentleness was gone. The velvet glove, Abigail thought, encased in Border steel.

'No.' Faith was vanquished. Sir Humphrey favoured her with a wolfish smile. 'I shall be interested to meet the young man. I never had a son – '

Geoffrey sat up as if aware of secret implications. For years, he had lived here, his mother in charge of the household affairs, almost a brother to Charity and Hope, and now he was threatened most subtly by the unexpected advent of a man no one had met. Who might succeed in winning Sir Humphrey's approval. The widow, it appeared, had already done so.

Abigail looked forward quite keenly to the following evening. But, sensing the disappointment of Charity's aunt, she addressed herself to Faith more out of kindness than of any real urge to know her better, aware all the time of an incipient excitement that was as much aroused by the anticipation of supping with the mysterious Rutherfords as by the tensions around this more than adequately equipped table. The food was better than she had expected. Mrs Davison, true Pringle or not, was a good housekeeper and deserved her place in this house.

The talk returned to the more famous of the Border Reivers. Scott of Harden, Buccleuch, Gibbie of the Gowden Garters, Jamie Telfer, the Flower of Yarrow, Jock Elliot; there seemed no end to the picturesque characters spawned in the no-man's-land between England and the Highlands. And then a hairy hand thrust forward the decanters of port and brandy aggressively so the women had, perforce, to rise and leave the room rather like recalcitrant children, Abigail mused ruefully.

Aunt Faith, in spite of Abigail's endeavours to be friendly, swept off towards her room and Hope escaped, a brown shadow on the stair, swiftly gone.

'What on earth do your father and Geoffrey have to say to one another?' Abigail asked as she and Charity went back to the red and white withdrawing-room.

'Nothing,' Charity replied, taking the same white-covered chair and allowing her legs to dangle over the arm. She made an attractive picture, her fair hair strewn across the geranium-coloured cushion, the velvet making a foil for the silky strands. 'Father offers Geoff a cigar which he invariably refuses. I believe the weather is mentioned, the state of the fields for hunting, the presence of moles on the lower pasture and the necessity for traps, then Geoff excuses himself and leaves Father to the ministrations of Hod Pringle. Hod takes Geoff's seat and they drink together. They never say a great deal. I listened once or twice, but the silence was more companionable than that of any family gathering.'

'A soldier becomes used to the company of men.'

'Geoffrey's a man.'

'But he isn't someone you've fought with and suffered with, someone who knows all your dead comrades. A man who knows the essential you.'

'I suppose not. But Father talks to Hope more than he does me. You'd never believe it because they are so different but I believe they are friends. Not me, of course.'

'Why of course? Does that mean you know why?'

Charity sighed. 'Yes.' Her face was suddenly white and pinched. She hunched her shoulders. 'I was responsible for the accident.'

'Which accident?'

'The one that killed Mother.'

'Oh, no – '

'Oh, yes. I was disobedient and Father could never forgive that. His army upbringing, you see. A man gives an order and it's immediately discharged or heaven help the person who fails to obey. We were never allowed to play in the drive for fear of being involved in an accident with incoming traffic. But you know what they say about forbidden fruit. I was in the rhododendrons when I heard my parents come back from the hunt. I ran out and – and – ' She swallowed nervously, obviously unhappy.

'Don't torture yourself – ' Abigail was disturbed.

'No, I must finish. It exorcizes things that build up in me. Just for a moment I saw them laughing together. Father was on Sultan – he was called that because he served all the mares at Duncraw and they used to amuse themselves about his harem. Mother had Susy, a little white mare. And then the picture changed. Susy and Sultan reared and Mother fell. Then Sultan's hooves came down on her. He was destroyed. And Father has never said a kind word to me since. Oh, he's perfectly polite but who wants courtesy? He sent me off to school as though he could no longer bear the sight of me. I thought the years away might have changed everything but they haven't. His leaves all coincided, purposely I always suspect, with term-time and it wasn't good for me to miss schooling. And the school was too far away to be accessible during his short spell at Duncraw. So we just never met. No one ever said to me, "It was your fault," but it was made obvious in other ways. It was my fault, of course, wasn't it? It was a stupid thing to do – '

'But you were a child. You didn't mean it – '

'Hope is like Mother. They were very close to one another. I was more exuberant in those days. The world was an exciting place. Mother looked more like Hope's elder sister. She was a small woman.'

'I'm sure your father's forgotten long since. He probably does not realize how you feel.'

'He doesn't want me to be happy.'

'Charity!'

'It's true. All of a sudden I knew I could not bear to be here all summer with them without the presence of someone who liked me and did not hold it against me that I once made a dreadful mistake.'

The firelight shivered against the glossy white paint and reflected itself in the silken embroidery of a small screen.

'I don't know what to say. I intend to prove you wrong if it's the last thing I do. But you've forgotten

Geoffrey, haven't you? He likes you. And your aunt does not object. I should say she favours a match strongly – '

"Opportunism,' Charity said flatly. 'Aunt Faith likes her position here and think how much stronger it would be if she were my mother-in-law.'

'Are you sure Geoffrey isn't in love with you?'

'I could never be sure, could I? In any case I am not in love with him so the question of marriage does not arise.'

'Then you must forget all about it. No one can drag you to church against your will.'

'People have ways of imposing their will,' Charity answered.

'I think it is just as well you invited me. I may be able to make you see that perhaps you are over sensitive – '

'I know I am not.'

'But you admit you have feelings of guilt?'

'Yes.'

'They can colour events.'

'I suppose so. Let us talk of something else. Have there been any men in your life?'

'None that mattered.'

'I'm surprised. You have so much. Your colouring alone – '

'You would be surprised how many people shy away from red hair. There are all kinds of old wives' tales associated with it. A fisherman would refuse to put to sea if he met me first thing in the morning.'

'You are not serious!'

'I am. It has happened to me. I'm an early riser and I love lonely beach walking. I once kept the fishing-fleet in port for an entire day while on holiday.'

Charity was laughing again, all her pretty teeth exposed. 'I'm glad you came. You won't go too soon? I should hate that.'

'You asked me that before. There are no pressing calls on my time. I had no one but Mother and Father. No sisters, brothers, cousins. Only my school friends and most of those are now settled and scattered abroad. There's only you who have kept in touch. The others promised and forgot.'

'Poor Abby.'

'Poor nothing! I am perfectly self-reliant.' Abigail stretched luxuriously then saw herself reflected in the over-mantel mirror, her body clearly defined in the forest-green gown, her skin white in contrast. She would be an acquired taste for most men, she realized, for she was not pretty in the approved sense, just colourful and arresting, both qualities that could be an embarrassment to the conventional. But who hankered after the conformist? Certainly not she. She wanted humour and spirit and, of course, total involvement. There was no place for half measures or apathy in her scheme of things.

'You always remind me of Becky in Thackeray's *Vanity Fair*.'

'Oh, thank you very much!' Abigail cried.

'It was meant as a compliment. She was so vital. I cannot bear sterility.'

'No.'

'And you are much nicer than Becky Sharp.'

'Oh, do not try to redeem yourself. Could we go out, do you think? Just for half an hour?'

'I did not like to suggest it after your journey but I do confess I myself feel house-bound. Fetch your cape and we'll go up the hill.' Charity's voice came alive.

'Very well. I can find my way upstairs. We'll meet down in the hall, shall we?'

It was good to see Charity cheerful again. Abigail went for her cape and found Charity, shawled and bright-eyed. Almost too gay, Abigail thought with misgivings. The poor girl seemed so repressed one moment, then extravagantly bright over a suggestion that they take the evening air in a setting that, for her, could hold no more surprises.

It was cooler outside and the trees were tossing gently. Strands of hair were blown over Abigail's face and she detached them carefully. Charity's eyes were everywhere, almost as though she expected to see someone. They passed a man in knee-breeches and gaiters and his features betrayed him for a Pringle. He bared his teeth briefly and passed on, an old fowling-piece tucked firmly under his arm.

'What is he looking for?' Abigail whispered.

'Youngs, naturally.' Charity was flippant, her profile curiously touching.

'I will *not* ask who the Youngs are,' Abigail said. 'I would rather wait and find out for myself.'

They left the trees that lined a low wall and she saw that the terraces were edged with worn pink marble that shut off outcroppings of rosebay willow-herb and rampant buttercups. The ground rose in heathery moorland then merged into thick woods that enclosed them, thick and silent as a blanket, their feet stirring up old beechmast and brown pine-needles, filling the air with scents of antiquity. 'How peaceful it is,' Abigail murmured, restored. 'How you must love it.'

'Oh, I do,' Charity answered. 'I should not like to see it pass to another.'

'There's no fear of that, is there? Only you and your sister. I heard your father say – he had no son.'

'He seems very taken with la Rutherford.'

'But liking does not always lead to other things.'

'She is an exceptional woman. And he has been without a wife for a long time. Now that his army life is ended, Father is more – motiveless. He's not too old to become a father to a second family.'

'Well, I do not know the intricacies of the situation as you do but a man who can remain a bachelor for so long is unlikely to throw away freedom so easily. He is no fool.'

'No. But he had great happiness with Mother. And Mrs Rutherford is clever. She could conjure up some – renewal.'

'Who is she?' Abigail toiled up a slope between tufts of bracken and heather roots. The edge of the Scott graveyard was now only a few hundred yards away and she saw the top half of a grey cross, the shadow slanted down the hill.

'A widow who has rented a house outside Peebles, close to Neidpath Peel. No one knows a great deal about her. I did not even know she had a child.'

'Is she – ?'

'Attractive? I think her rather forceful but that would be a virtue in Father's eyes.'

'Do not worry before there is need. At present she is only a supper guest.'

'He finds her exciting.'

'I find circuses exciting but I would not want to introduce them into my house.'

'Oh, dear Abby. You are so eminently comforting. But you'll see – '

They panted towards the graveyard gate, which stood open. Charity frowned. 'It should be kept shut. The sheep get in and tread on the graves. Overset the flower-vases.'

'Where's your mother buried?'

'Over there. The west wall.'

'Shall we look?'

'If you like.'

'They *are* all Scotts and Pringles. I did not quite believe it,' Abigail observed, watching the shadows of leaves against the mildewed stones. 'And that, I suppose, is the chapel?'

'Yes. The minister comes for occasional services and for births, weddings, christenings, funerals – '

'How very feudal.' Abigail was intrigued. There were not quite so many graves as she had expected. It seemed that both families were long lived. Katherine Scott, David Pringle. But now Elizabeth, Mary and Margaret Scott, two, three and four years respectively. What heartache to be contained on one slab of granite. James Scott, eighteen years old, killed at Copenhagen. He would have belonged to the Naval branch of the family. Poor little midshipman. Ewan Pringle – lost at Trafalgar. Joseph Pringle, cut down by shrapnel at Waterloo, and cheek by jowl with young Sir Geoffrey Scott who died in the same battle. Another Richard and Blondell, Abigail thought compassionately, her eye recording more infant deaths and mothers not surviving the birth of a child. Two deaths from cholera –

'There's Mother's,' Charity said, pointing. 'You go. I'll be waiting outside.'

Abigail hesitated.

'There is no reason why you shouldn't look,' Charity went on gently. 'I do not wish to. Not at this moment – '

'All right.' It was obvious Charity wanted to be alone and Abigail was curious. She went forward, her feet silent on the moss that encroached upon the path and wreathed the bases of the old stones. She was almost on top of the grave before she saw Hope. The girl was kneeling, her hands together, head bowed.

Abigail stopped, waiting, not wishing to intrude, nor wanting to disturb the girl's prayer.

'He should not want to put another in your place,' Hope said in a low voice. 'It is you he loves. That woman influences him too much. He should never try to replace you. Mama? Mama! I miss you, all the time.' She flung herself forward on to the short grass that covered her mother's resting-place and, for a moment, her arms outstretched at either side, took the form of a brown cross.

Abigail stepped back, her gaze encompassing the text on the Celtic stone. 'For Johanne Wilson Scott, died the fourth day of April 1854, beloved wife of Humphrey Scott. Ever remembered.'

Hope remained where she was and, after a moment, Abigail turned and made her way back to the gate. Something moved across the hill, and, peering hard, she thought she made out the shape of a horseman a long way off. A man in a grey cloak.

She slept fitfully. The bed was strange and she had never been comfortable the first night away from home. Again she imagined she heard voices, very low and vaguely acrimonious, but it could have been the sound of the wind which seemed to have risen. A man in grey galloped across a stark landscape scattered with crosses all bearing the initial S.

It was a relief when morning came. The world beyond the window was a soft haze of grey, the outlines of hill and garden blurred. Moisture slid down the window pane and there was a sigh of disturbance down the chimney, a spatter of damp soot in the grate. The painted wallpaper filled the room with a soft green glow.

The moustached maid came with a cup of chocolate, her glum expression unchanging as she surveyed the feminine disorder of stays and petticoats, the green dress flung across a chair-back. 'I'll fetch some hot water, miss.'

'Thank you,' Abigail said, snuggling against the pillow. 'You'll be busy today with visitors expected.'

A spark of life came into the lack-lustre eyes. 'Yes, miss.'

'Thank you, – ?'

'Jeannie, miss.'

'Jeannie. You know Mrs Rutherford?'

'Only to look at. But I must not hang about, Miss Menory. Mrs Davison would not care for it. I'll get the washing water.'

Abigail, feeling decidedly snubbed, watched her retreating back. Pringles owed loyalty and pleasantness only to Scotts. They disapproved of quizzing by strangers. She supposed it was in their favour but a gossip now and again was both agreeable and instructive and she would love to know whether Charity and Hope were prejudiced in their opinion of the widow. Few children cared for the usurpation of a mother's place. But surely their memories of Johanne Scott would be tempered by distance? It seemed not to be so where Hope was concerned.

Sheep bawled from the hill, breaking her train of thought. She climbed out of bed and began to brush her hair with long smooth strokes, her reflection a little eerie in the verdant gloom.

Once ready, she was disinclined to stay upstairs. Quietly, she went down the staircase, her hand gliding over the dark rail. She could hear Sir Humphrey's voice upraised in a kind of anger. 'I tell you, Hod. There are several things missing. I know I rarely pay attention to what's in the house. Bits and pieces have never had importance for me. But I'll not be robbed. It was the books I noticed first. They'd been replaced by others but the symmetry of the shelves was spoiled. So that's why I've sent for a private detective. And a photographer.'

'Photographer?' Hod seemed understandably puzzled.

'Collectors have begun to have their treasures photographed. It's an official record. An insurance against theft. And if the worst happens there's a picture for Scotland Yard. It can be duplicated and sent to a number of towns. Could catch the thieves red-handed.'

'I don't hold with taking folks' likenesses,' Hod growled. 'Never did. Never will.'

'Superstition. What harm can it do?'

'It'll be unlucky. Who do you think took these things? Not one of us.' His tone suggested outrage.

'Not you, Hod, certainly. I detest the idea of it being anybody. However, this new inventory will show up anything that vanishes, or a substitution. Never cared for being duped. You see, I've a good idea of order. Years of inspecting men and equipment sharpened my eye. One gets used to a thing being in a certain place. It's a mechanical reflex.'

Abigail's foot slipped on the edge of a step and she clattered to the stained boards of the hall. 'Oh, dear,' she said. 'How careless of me.'

Sir Humphrey appeared, frowning. 'Oh, it's you, Miss Menory. You're not hurt?'

'I was looking for the withdrawing-room. I thought I might find Charity there.'

Her host looked at her, obviously wondering how much she had overheard. Abigail decided to take the bull by the horns. 'I could not help hearing what you said. The house is so quiet. It – was not intended.'

'We do not usually have guests rise so early. But it's no secret. I shall be telling the others today. The arrival of the photographic people and an investigator could hardly pass unnoticed and rooms must be got ready. I said nothing last night because you were there and I wished not to embarrass a stranger. However, what's done is done.' He shrugged.

'I'm sorry.'

'My dear Miss Menory, there's nothing to apologize for. I'm a compulsive early riser myself so why should I condemn you? Just forget my problems and we'll say no more.'

'Very well.'

'Now the withdrawing-room is on your left. You'll find some news-sheets – out-of-date I fear – and a shelf of books under the window. You strike me as a bookish young lady in spite of a certain spiritedness I admire. I do not suppose Charity will be long in following you. She will be conscientious with a guest in the house.' Sir Humphrey smiled and looked very attractive. This house and his looks would make him much sought after, Abigail reflected, wanting more than ever to see the disruptive widow.

'Oh, and Miss Menory, I almost forgot. We gather for a Bible reading and prayers on Sunday mornings. If you would care to join us at eleven?'

'I should.' It would be interesting to discover his choice of a text.

The white room with its splashes of geranium and black, its sombre portraits, had a welcome warmth. A fire burned already in the shining grate and struck glints from the brass handles of an oak chest near the window, and the gilt tooling on the half-dozen books on the white-painted shelf. She crossed the red carpet with its squares of dull gold incorporating a design of peacock-blue, and took one of the books. It was Mrs Gaskell's *Cranford*, a favourite of hers. There was a great deal of excitement in the Gaskell stories which lifted them from the more ordinary; press-gangs and witch-hunts, haunting and unquiet deaths. Abigail despised herself frequently for her addition to sensation. Not for the first time she envied Charity her cool reserve. A quality, she remembered, that had not been acquired without pain.

The train of thought took Abigail back to the moment when Hope had cast herself down on her mother's grave, and produced a flicker of revulsion. Something screamed close by.

'Oh, there you are!' Charity said unexpectedly. Abigail started. 'How nervous you seem to be.'

'How quiet you are,' Abigail retaliated. 'Didn't you hear that scream?'

'What scream?'

'A most unpleasant sound. Like – someone having their throat cut.'

'And how many times have you been present at such an event?' Charity drifted, draped in palest lilac, across the floor.

Abigail laughed.

'Now, what about breakfast?'

'Shouldn't we wait for the rest of the household?'

'Everyone comes when they will.' Charity shrugged. 'Father has his at crack of dawn as though he were on a campaign and must draw up his battle-plan before sun-up.'

'I – have already seen him.'

'And he invited you to prayers?'

'Yes. I accepted.'

'Sometimes I feel decidedly un-Christian. It seems hypocritical to kneel and mouth platitudes.'

'Come, Charity. No self-pity or pessimism.'

'Of course not. I'll drive you away. If only you knew – '

'Well, I am not likely to do that if you don't tell me.' Abigail looked at her keenly.

'I will – later.'

'Good. Then let us eat.'

They ate a leisurely meal with the soothing sound of soft rain against the pane, the whisper of the fire. Kidneys, bacon, eggs and sausages reposed under silver covers on a long carved sideboard. A golden-haired Scott stared down from either end of the room. Afterwards Charity went away for keys and began to show Abigail around the still quiet house.

They peeped in an enormous kitchen, all scrubbed tables, huge glazed crocks and copper pans, populated not unexpectedly by dark-faced Pringle women, even the youngest of whom showed traces of dark hair on their upper lips. Put them into men's clothing and they would not have looked out of place.

There was a flagged wash-house, a little brewery and what looked suspiciously like a still, a cool dairy, an ice-pit, a storehouse where sides of beef and mutton hung, then a dark stone stair that echoed, emerging on to the ground floor of the house. A small morning-room opened out, the fire smoking a little and hazing the greenish walls, a door that led to the house-keeper's sitting-room was ignored, then came a very pretty closet filled with china set out on shelves, more Scott portraits and remarkably little else but a carpet.

"It's *famille-rose*," Charity said, indicating the china. 'Some cracked, unfortunately. I expect it will appear this evening. It does for guests of importance.' Her voice was edged with distaste.

'Now, Charity. You promised me earlier, no despondency.'

Charity made an effort. 'It's just so unfair. That some may and some may not – '

'You are speaking in riddles.'

'Oh, come and see the bedrooms!'

'Including the one next to mine?'

Charity smiled with the faintest trace of malice. 'Including that.'

The nursery contained a fine oaken cradle, heavily carved and set upon rockers; prim beds with starched white counterpanes being in sharp contrast to the one in the next chamber where the bed was enormous and resembled nothing so much as a galleon in full sail, yellow, embroidered with black and white. Abigail was greatly impressed. What a bed to retire to with the man one loved. It would make an occasion of something that should be splendid and unforgettable.

None of the other sleeping apartments was comparable with the magnificence of the yellow chamber and Abigail found the rest an anti-climax. So it was with a shock that she stared into the room that had been locked and from which had issued the sounds of muted conversation – or so she had thought.

The wall that faced her was entirely carved, the central portion, depicting a peacock with outspread tail, painted realistically in its true colours. The bird and the wide fan of its tail formed the head of a great bed, the poles and base carved to match with peacock eyes and heads, the delicate coronets reminding Abigail of the gipsy's words. Royal birds. The peacock crowns were kingly indeed. The blue-green hangings swayed gently in the draught from the open door. Peacock feathers in a turquoise vase twitched in unison.

'Well?' Charity enquired.

'It's – it's too much. Fantastic –'

'Everyone feels that way first time.'

'I suppose all kinds of people know about it?'

'Some. Why?'

'That gipsy knew. Or I think she did. She told me I'd see royal birds.'

Again Charity frowned. 'We do not like too many knowing. It could be a temptation.'

'But no one could bypass your Pringles, could they?'

'It has been known. A long time ago. It's an unlucky bed, you see. One Scott bride at least went to sleep in it and was gone next morning, the door locked.'

The hangings stirred.

'Could she not have locked it after her and run away?'

'The key was on the inside.'

'And no one saw her again?'

'Not alive. She was taken out of the stream some days later, floating like Ophelia – '

'It's a story, isn't it? Invented for credulous guests.'

'It's true,' Charity said in a faraway voice. 'Quite true.'

Something screamed and the sound reverberated through the room.

TWO

'There it is again,' Abigail said, shaken. 'Surely you heard this time?'

'Oh, yes. It's a peacock. A real one. They have a pen in the garden. I expect Hod has let them out.'

'To think that such a beautiful bird could be responsible for such a discordant sound.'

'I never think about it. We have always had them. They become part of the background.' Charity crossed to the window and peered out. 'It seems to have stopped raining. Would you like to see them for yourself?'

'Yes. Is that why you lock the room? Because of the girl who disappeared?'

'Partly. But mainly so that the carving is not damaged. It's a show-piece.'

Abigail went to inspect the view for herself. Any idea that the missing girl might have left by the window vanished instantly. The wall plunged sheer to a shadowy tangle of shrubs, and there had been no mention of knotted sheets or of a rope.

'Do you believe it?'

'Yes. There are authenticated records. She even has a grave on the hill, not far from – from Mother's. Her name was Felicity Croser. She certainly existed.'

'I suppose it was a long time ago?'

'It happened in 1746. Giles Scott returned from

Culloden not long before and wanted to marry in case he was forced into exile as a Stuart sympathizer. When Felicity was found dead he went of his own accord and that was the last heard of him. The house came to his younger brother, Martin. It was concluded Giles had gone to France to join Prince Charles Edward and had been killed in his service. Or perhaps he did not wish to return to be reminded of her. Or he may even have taken his own life.'

'Poor young man. But there must be a logical explanation. For Felicity Croser's disappearance.'

'You are such a determinedly reasonable person, my dear Abigail. Wouldn't you secretly prefer it to be some kind of witchcraft?'

'I would, but a cold little voice keeps telling me there's no such thing.'

'It's a pity. You'd have made a fascinating witch.'

'Really! Becky Sharp – witches. I begin to wonder why I came.'

'You make insults out of compliments. You must know you are the most exciting-looking person ever to come out of that constricting school of ours. A red and white woman studded with bits of green glass for eyes – '

'There, you see! I must even have glass eyes, not emeralds.' Abigail chuckled.

'Emeralds are too dark. Green glass is just right.'

Abigail opened her mouth to retort then was stopped by the raucous screech of one of the birds in the garden. She strained her eyes to see the peacock but there was nothing to be seen but a blur of wet shrubbery and a suggestion of pallid movement beyond.

'Charity,' Sir Humphrey said from the doorway. 'You will keep Miss Menory from prayers.'

The two girls spun around guiltily. Abigail recovered first from the shock. 'It was I kept her. We lost count of the hours in your timeless house. I could not see enough of it. Your daughter is blameless.'

'You have liked what you have seen?'

'It is splendid.'

'Give me the keys, then, Charity. I will see this room safely locked.'

'I – ' Charity began, flushing, but her father cut her short with a brusque 'I prefer to do it myself. I shall need the keys later, when Mrs Rutherford arrives. She has heard of the Peacock Bed and is anxious to see it. I will see you both in the dining-room.' It was a definite dismissal.

'Damn Mrs Rutherford and her obnoxious son!' Charity whispered as they went downstairs again.

'How do you know he's obnoxious?' Abigail murmured. 'None of you has met him.'

'He is bound to be.'

'Look on the bright side!' Abigail chided. 'Optimism is so much more positive.'

'But that is the whole reason for our friendship. The attraction of opposites. You are assured. I am not. And I know I shall find Father's prayers a sad trial. He manifests a Christianity I fear he does not feel. How so hard and unyielding a man could have two such daughters I have never understood – '

'Hush, Charity!' Abigail said nervously. 'The sound of voices carries upstairs, as I know to my cost.' They had reached the hall and the spot where, earlier, she had almost fallen.

'Oh! And what is that supposed to mean?' Charity looked curious.

'I think everyone is assembled,' Abigail said with a look through the doorway. 'It must be explained later.'

Once inside the room they were surrounded by

Pringles. Abigail felt like Mary, Queen of Scots on the way to execution. These strong, dark people oppressed her with their suggestion of being jailers. Geoffrey looked hang-dog, yet contrived to sit next to an unwilling Charity. Aunt Faith stared ahead with eyes of china that melted occasionally when they rested upon the magnificent sideboard or a particularly fine branch of silver candlesticks. Hope merged into the shadows in the corner, only her eyes and the small, jet buttons on her tight, narrow bodice catching glints of feeble light. Apart from Charity, there was little colour about the assembly, and Abigail, in her green dress and riot of red hair, felt distinctly obtrusive like some gaudy parrot in a cage of sparrows. Not that one could ever really connect Pringles with such homely birds. They were — crows and buzzards. Predators —

Sir Humphrey appeared, his gaze approving the waiting congregation, a fugitive beam of watery light outlining the magnificently leonine head, Hod Pringle following him, closing the door.

Abigail, fascinated by the phalanxes of black dresses and white aprons, the caps bent at a submissive angle as though each knelt in private fealty to their great golden lord finally returned from heathenish places, the scowling faces of Pringle men, became aware that Sir Humphrey singled out from the rest his daughter Charity.

The prayers began and then he opened the big, black Bible and began to read in a clear, concise voice that contained only a trace of a Scots accent. The years abroad had removed his dialect almost completely.

'And Adam knew Eve, his wife, and she conceived and bore Cain,' Sir Humphrey began and paused while Charity's eyes were suddenly raised to his. A wave of hostility seemed to pass between them. Cruel, Abigail thought helplessly. She had not really believed Charity and her tales of Sir Humphrey's unforgiving attitude, but intuition told her that this text was for his daughter's benefit. He did still hold it against the girl that she had been the cause of Johanne Scott's undeniably tragic accident. So had Johanne borne her own death.

The crisp, business-like voice went on, terribly clear. Abigail listened, hating him.

'And it came to pass, when they were in the field, that Cain rose up against Abel his brother and slew him.

'And the Lord said unto Cain, "Where is Abel, thy brother?" And he said, "I know not. Am I my brother's keeper?"

'And He said, "What hast thou done? The voice of thy brother's blood crieth unto me from the ground." '

So too the blood of Johanne as she lay on the drive under those merciless hooves.

' "And now are thou cursed from the earth which hath opened her mouth to receive thy brother's blood from thy hand." ' How skilfully he stressed the 'thy'.

Sir Humphrey's voice had grown soft but equally penetrating. 'And Cain said unto the Lord, "My punishment is greater than I can bear – " '

Charity got up and blundered towards the door. Pringle eyes followed her progress with what seemed like dark approval.

'Where are you going?' Her father's voice crackled as though he addressed misbehaving troops who must be brought to heel.

She did not answer, only went out of the room, her steps sharp on the flagged passage. Abigail rose to her feet, her gaze accusing. 'I will go with her.'

'Prayers are not finished, Miss Menory.'

'No matter. I beg you to excuse me.' This time she

was the cynosure of all those implacable looks. Her cheeks flushed. Hope was watching her with guarded interest and Geoffrey with a sulkiness engendered most probably by the knowledge that he would not have dared do anything so decisive and resented the realization. Faith frowned.

'Very well. If you are set on going. But I warn you, Charity seeks only attention.'

And love, and reassurance, Abigail longed to cry out, but bit back her words. 'She may be unwell and there is no one to attend to her,' she said quietly.

'As you will.'

There was a silence as she left. Outside, the house lay quiet. There was no way of knowing where Charity had gone. Behind her, Sir Humphrey had recommenced his reading and a hot anger consumed Abigail. The story was too near the bone, too close to the tragedy that had befallen the Scotts. She had a hot desire to take a stick to the Master of Duncraw for the streak of sadism he undoubtedly possessed. Yet, could one blame him entirely? His suffering must have been as great as he stared down at his wife's shattered body. His bitterness was understandable. But to take it out on a child who had never forgotten her own guilt seemed inhuman. Perhaps he imagined Charity had acted purposely. The mother seemed wrapped up in the younger child, Hope. The father was obsessed with the mother. No one had been over-concerned with Charity. Was it possible – ?

Abigail tried to shake off the premonition of worse things to come. She had almost reached her own room when Charity appeared, very white and rigid, and wearing a riding-habit. She stopped at the sight of her friend. 'You left.'

'I was anxious about you. Can I come too?'

'If you hurry. I do not wish to encounter my father

at present.' Charity gripped the small riding-switch tighter, and scowled.

'Two minutes.'

Abigail was as good as her word. She said nothing of what had just transpired, only flung herself into her own habit and pulled a hard hat over her hair. They met no one, not even in the stables, then Abigail remembered that all the Pringles were still indoors, a captive audience.

They saddled two mares, Charity's white and Abigail's a chestnut called Suzy, and began to trot down the winding drive, the drops of rain falling on to their shoulders in a desultory fashion. Once past the gates, Charity turned to the left and began to follow the pink wall. A great bank of firs gloomed down on them from the other side of the track but a vague glimmer in the sky betokened an improvement in the weather.

'Will no one object if we are not there for luncheon?' Abigail enquired.

'There's little or no cooking done on summer Sunday mornings because of the service. A cold table is always available.'

'That is convenient.'

'Oh, poor Abby! Were you afraid you'd starve because of your championship?'

'I will admit to a certain fear and I cannot abide being hungry. It's my besetting sin.'

'No one would suspect it with that small waist. But you can look forward to a good dinner tonight.'

'Where are we going?' Abigail was aware of a certain purpose in Charity's dogged progress.

'Nowhere in particular. This is a prettier route than the other side of Duncraw.'

The firs were petering out to reveal the typical shapes of Border hills that seemed, to Abigail, to be unlike any other hills she had ever seen. Round yet wild, not unfriendly, yet stark and bare but for the circles of sheep folds and sudden disconcerting outcrops of abandoned towers, roofless and eyeless, harbouring birds and shadows. That was what the gipsy had said. Shadows –

The peel rose from the side of a stony bed where water gushed noisily between tough, reedy banks. 'Shall we look?' Abigail asked, pulling Suzy to a standstill.

'Of course.' Charity sounded almost happy.

A shroud of mist hung about the old building, hazing the outlines. Stones rattled away as they toiled up the uneven track that led from a crumbled wall that had once enclosed the land on the opposite side of the beck they had crossed by slimy stepping-stones. Nettles and willowherb pressed against the rough base of the tower.

'Creepy,' Abigail said, raising her eyes to the blind windows. And then she froze into immobility. Someone was staring down from the dark space.

Charity was already inside the doorless gap, only a flicker of her dark habit and the heel of a boot still visible, then gone in the obscurity with a haste Abigail could not fathom.

'Charity!' she called in warning, then heard the clatter of footsteps on a stone stair. The face had gone as though it had never been. There was a silence in which nothing moved, then two white butterflies floated past Abigail's face like bits of live paper, bringing her back to reality. She almost ran up the now-dangerous steps and found herself in a dank dimness of broken masonry out of which rose narrow steps curving out of sight. Quietly, she ascended, her fingertips rubbing against the chill grittiness of sandstone that made them tingle.

A small, grey chamber opened out before her, not much light coming through the long, narrow slits that were the windows. Charity was there, caught in the arms of a tall man in riding-breeches and a grey coat. He raised his head and said, 'You are early.'

'I walked out of Father's prayer-meeting.'

'Why?' Both were unaware of her presence.

'He reminded me of a mistake I once made. In front of everyone. And Geoff looked censorious or I imagined he did and that added fuel – Oh, Colin. If it were not for Abigail, I'd run away! Oh – Abigail.' Charity detached herself from the close embrace.

'I'm glad you've remembered me,' Abigail said dryly. 'I imagined you'd run into danger.'

'No. Only into the arms of the man I love.' Charity laughed softly and the man Colin turned to show Abigail a brown, young face, grey-eyed and pleasant, and a head of curly brown hair that added to the impression of attractive youth.

'I take it,' Abigail said, 'that Sir Humphrey does not know?'

'I am forbidden to see Colin again. But if I am with you, he'll never know, will he?'

'Then – that was your reason for inviting me?' Abigail's voice changed.

'Oh, dear Abby! Not initially, I swear. What I told you was the truth. I needed someone in that unfriendly house. And you know yourself that if you'd not decided quite involuntarily to follow me, I'd have left Duncraw anyway, just in case Colin might have come today. It was you who asked to accompany me and I thought you'd understand.'

'Perhaps I do. But it places me in an uncomfortable position. What if your father should enquire where we go? What we do? Whom we encounter?'

'You must choose. And I'll think no ill of you, whatever you decide.'

'And who do I address?' Abigail asked of the stranger.

'Colin Crichton, of Cauldshiel. Our families are old enemies. That broken wall you came over was the boundary between our lands, a boundary disputed since pre-Tudor times. Our claim was upheld and the Scotts detested us for it.'

'And Father is implacable. He says the old judgement was unfair and that the Crichtons have always known this. A vendetta over a few miles of peat bogs and moor! If Colin and I were allowed, we'd heal the breach permanently.'

'You begin to sound like the Montagues and Capulets,' Abigail observed, still uncomfortable that she was part of a deception that could have major repercussions.

'That is not far from the truth,' Colin Crichton told her.

'You remember Felicity?' Charity said. 'Felicity Croser?'

'The bride who vanished from the Peacock Bed?'

'She was part-Crichton. That did not please your ancestors, did it, Colin?'

He shook his head. 'Neither the fact of the marriage, nor that of her burial on Scott ground.'

'Then – they were actually married?' Abigail murmured. 'I had the impression the girl was alone – probably on her wedding eve.'

'Giles was away, trying to arrange for them to sail together. He had to leave her while he went to Leith and back. He must have warned her to lock herself in. Another Romeo and Juliet. The Border was studded with such sad little liaisons,' Charity replied, her gaiety quenched. 'I dare say if Colin and I ran away, Father would follow us with his service pistol.'

'Or a heavenly thunderbolt,' Colin observed, rubbing some dirt from the sleeve of his grey coat. The colour made Abigail obscurely uneasy. She had not forgotten the gipsy's warning and here she was in this shadowy peel with a curly-haired Lochinvar dressed in grey. There was only one fly in the ointment. He was in love with Charity, or the girl thought he was. Somehow, Abigail must find out more about the Crichtons. Colin could be an adventurer trying to compromise a rich man's daughter. There could be no happiness as a result.

'How sacrilegious of you,' Charity told Colin. Neither made a move to go.

'I'll wait for you outside,' Abigail said. No one demurred.

She almost tripped on the way down. The edges of the curved stair were worn into hollows and it was dark. Beyond the black edge of the gaping doorway, the summer world looked impossibly bright. The butterflies had returned and flitted on to a group of harebells and some heads of pink clover. The sound of the stream grew louder as she stepped into the midday heat. No trace now of this morning's damp. The sun was bright.

She had gone only a few steps when she was confronted by a gaitered man who seemed to appear from nowhere. 'Who are you, miss?'

'My name is Menory, but what is it to you?'

'You're on Crichton land. That's what it is to me. I should take yourself off. That is your horse on the other bank?'

'Yes. But I do have a right to be here.'

The man's mouth twisted to one side. Cold eyes

bored into hers. His square, angled face intimidated her. 'From Duncraw, are you?'

'Yes, but – '

'Then you can take yourself over the burn as fast as your legs will take you. We've no truck wi' Scotts or their cronies. And the Hanging Tower is ours.'

'Your master?'

'Crichton o' Cauldshiel, as if you did not know.'

'Then you'll find him in the Hanging Tower as you so picturesquely call it. I have just left him there. Mr Colin, that is. Not that he will thank you for intruding,' she added hastily, remembering that Charity's presence would be speedily reported. She turned and called up towards the window. 'Colin! There's a man here wants to drive me off. I said you'd not want to be disturbed. Would you ask him not to pester me? I did come at your invitation.'

There was a pause, then Colin's face appeared at the slit. 'I'll thank you to go, Young. The young lady speaks the truth.'

'You know your father's orders,' the man growled.

'There is no harm done. She's a few feet into Cauldshiel only, because she wished to see the Hanging Tower. Now, be off with you, Young. I'll answer to my father. I'm sure you have more urgent calls on your time.' A coldness had infused Colin's tones and Abigail was startled by the change in him. He no longer looked young and charming. This man in grey had two sides to his nature.

The man went unwillingly, following the line of the wall.

Charity was framed, momentarily, against the gloom of the peel's interior, then she came down the steps in a more sober frame of mind. 'We will have to be even more careful, it seems. Still, you have given Young something to think about, Abby. Either he believes it was an unexpected meeting or he'll imagine Colin's given me up. The latter, more likely, since you called Colin by his Christian name and a stranger would have used his surname.'

'It's fortunate only one mare can be seen from this angle. Had there been two, he'd not have been fooled for a second. I suggest we go while your luck holds. I take it there are several Youngs?'

Charity nodded.

'And just as Scott and Crichton are eternally at loggerheads, so too the Youngs and Pringles?'

'Exactly. It is the Border, Abby, and the feuds do not die. The Highlands are as bad. There are still MacDonalds who'll spit on a Campbell's shadow.'

Abigail shook her head. 'None of this is what I expected —'

'But it grips you just the same?' Crichton suggested and Abigail knew it to be true.

'Yes. It grips. I fear it may take too great a hold on me. That I'll not want to go home.' Abigail was annoyed that she had been encouraged to put her new thoughts into words. 'But that's ridiculous. I have to go back. It's inevitable.'

'Only not yet,' Charity reminded. 'I want you here. I need you.'

'You make your own chains to bind me.'

'Then you *are* staying. That's good, isn't it, Colin?'

'Eminently,' he replied, and Abigail was sure she had not imagined the spark of excitement in his level gaze. Grey. Why must he wear that colour?'

Charity, her fair face flushed, took his hand briefly. 'Remember.'

'I will remember. Goodbye, Miss Menory.'

'Au revoir, Mr Crichton. I feel I have not seen the last of you.' Abigail went to traverse the slippery stones that crossed the contentious burn. She heard

Charity's soft secret laughter, then the sound of her feet on the makeshift ford, but when she looked back from the safety of the opposite bank Crichton had gone.

They were not too late for the remains of the cold lunch. Abigail waited uneasily for the advent of Sir Humphrey to upbraid them both. If he did, she would have to speak her mind and that would be the end of a stay that became increasingly interesting, if at times disquieting. But who wanted limitless calm? Better by far to be stimulated, even provoked.

She and Charity had their lunch in peace, then went out on to the terrace to search for the peacocks. Hod Pringle was there, smoking a clay pipe, his fowling-piece propped up within reach. He had been occupied with topiary and the snippings lay around his feet in green mounds. The birds were not immediately visible. Pillars hung with tendrils of ivy held up a long roof of glass, and Charity, with a nod to Pringle, began to walk under this canopy, her skirt sweeping the flags.

A raucous scream rent the air and Abigail, in spite of half-expecting the sound, jerked involuntarily. The next moment, the peacock appeared, flirting his long tail into a seductive fan, his delicate crown shining. A peahen followed submissively, well aware of her own ordinariness.

'That's Hamlet,' Charity said, enjoying Abigail's fright. 'And she's Ophelia, poor little dear. So humble and Uriah Heepish. Too many a woman's lot, I fear.'

'Are there others?'

'Yes.'

'Then how do you know them apart?'

'When you live with creatures you do know. I disbelieve the theory that all pigs or cows look alike. Anyway, Hamlet is always the noisiest, like an actor, declaiming – '

'Whatever is that?' Abigail asked, halting. 'Not Mrs Rutherford arriving? It seems far too early for a dinner guest.'

'It is. We do not expect anyone. Let's go and look through the shrubbery.' Charity giggled like a mischievous child and vanished through a gap in the topiary. Abigail had, perforce, to go after her.

'Do you think,' she panted, disengaging her sleeve from a trailing branch, 'that the Youngs have gone berserk and are converging on the Pringles? A last definitive engagement?'

Charity put back her head and laughed joyously. 'I do hope it may be! What on *earth* is it? The ground quakes.'

They stopped short between two tall rhododendrons watching the juggernaut approach of a pair of white shire horses dragging an enormous black-covered van, its sides bearing the legend, 'Martin's Photographic Carriage', in gold and purple letters. A stolid coachman handled the reins, his plump cheeks red-veined.

'But – it's gigantic! Do you suppose he has lost his way?' Charity asked, bemused.

'I imagine so,' Abigail began, then remembered the conversation between Hod and Sir Humphrey early this morning. 'Well – I don't know. We should let him go to the house, in case your father – '

'But why should Father – ? Oh, I wonder if he plans to have portraits taken of *her*? Madame Rutherford and her son. I told you he was very struck with her.'

'Why should he not have decided to photograph you and Hope?'

'He'd not want a picture of me!'

'Now, *how* do you know? This could be extremely diverting.' The great well-kept beasts had thundered by and there was a sighting of occupancy through a gap at the back of the vehicle, a broad tweed-covered back, then a glimpse of a face, a long, dark Stuart face with hooded eyes and black side-burns. So might Charles the Second have appeared, Abigail thought, staring after the careering conveyance and imagining the flutter in the dovecote that was bound to ensue.

Black, Stuart eyes suddenly clashed with her own. A head and shoulders protruded recklessly. An arm gesticulated. 'Duncraw?' he called out.

'Yes!' Abigail shouted, aware that her hair had fallen down in the wild stampede through the shrubs and hung around her in complete disarray. The man waved his thanks, dislodging folds of a flamboyant cape in dark grey. The black, Spanish-style hat added to what she privately considered to be a studiedly artistic appearance. The man in tweeds did not turn, being occupied with the contents of the van to the exclusion of all else.

Charity giggled again. 'That, I presume, was Mr Martin. A presentable person. As you say, a diversion would be welcome. Father can hardly take me to task with the house so unexpectedly full of people. At least two in the photographic van. Two more this evening.' Charity's feet scuffed at the gravel in her efforts to arrive at the porch at the same time as the van. The high, rounded roof was reminiscent of the wagons used by the American pioneers. The long, dark face of Martin still showed in the opening, intelligent, promising amusement above the normal level. He could be the perfect antidote to the aura of grievance and dislike Abigail had been forced to accept during her short stay. Photography was so fascinating. A box and tripod, a head under a black cloth, an interval, then a likeness that was a miracle.

The area around the front of the house was, by now, thick with Pringles. Mrs Davison had come on to the step, an assortment of maids peeping out behind her, or with noses pressed to windows. Footmen, boot-boys and, heading everyone else, Hod in his position of seniority, had confronted the van threateningly or with interest.

The coachman sat where he was, ignoring the hubbub that had been caused by their arrival. The flap of the van was flung open to reveal a mass of equipment and boxes and the ill-natured scowl of the tweed-suited and hatted man. Martin sprang down, extravagant in wide-brimmed hat and cloak, and made a low, actorish bow that secretly delighted Abigail while she took herself to task yet again for her penchant for the theatrical. Charity could not refrain from smiling and the black, laughing eyes were appreciative.

'I thought I should never find the place,' Martin said in a pleasant Scots voice. It was not as broad or harsh as the Pringle or Young dialect but distinctly un-English. 'Now I'd be obliged if you would tell Sir Humphrey that Mr Kenith Martin has arrived. Oh – and Inspector Moray. I met him at the road end. His horse had gone lame and I think he would be obliged if a man would go down to attend the poor brute. It's tethered to an elm.'

'Sir Humphrey expects you today?' Hod Pringle growled.

'Well – er, no, it was tomorrow, but I am notoriously bad with the calendar. I hate time, dates and that sort of thing. So I set out thinking this was my day for Duncraw and I apologize most humbly for putting my particular cat among the pigeons.' He favoured Mrs Davison with a look that would have melted stone and

55

set her bridling with a pink pleasure. 'We should not expect much but for the safe housing of the van which contains irreplaceable equipment, attention for these stalwart friends –' he flicked the nearest horse – 'and some bread and cheese for the Inspector and myself.'

'I'll take you to Father,' Charity told him. 'I am Miss Scott.'

'Well.' The amused gaze went from Charity to Abigail. 'And?'

'And that is my friend, Abigail Menory.'

'I am delighted to meet you. Come, Inspector. Our possessions are, I can see, in excellent hands. The trunk and the leather bag are to be brought to our respective rooms. Nothing else to be moved a fraction of an inch. Is that clear?'

'Quite clear,' Hod replied grumpily and gestured to three Pringles who might have been cast in the identical mould and attacking Charity's theory against homogeneity.

Charity and the two travellers passed into the hall, Abigail lagging behind. No two men could have been more dissimilar, Martin tall and elegant, totally extrovert, Moray broad and frowning, square of hand and foot, not to mention beard, obviously ill at ease. But policemen had a right to view the world through jaundiced eyes, Abigail reflected, half-aware of various female Pringles darting hither and thither from their grandstand view of the stylish arrival and the annoyed cluck-clucks of Mrs Davison as she stepped inside.

Charity was obviously bound for Sir Humphrey's study, so Abigail went into the withdrawing-room and pretended to begin Ruskin's *Stones of Venice*, a book that at any other time would have drawn her like a magnet, but which at this moment remained a jumble of words out of which observations jumped every so often like trout at mayflies.

'Oh, there you are.' Charity's eyes were gleaming. 'You've no idea of the secrecy of the whole thing. Father turned quite red when he saw them and they were whisked in and the door closed before you could say "snap". I tried to hear what was said but it's a very thick, close-fitting door and all that emerged was a low grumble, I wish I knew what it was all about.'

Abigail was silent. She could have enlightened Charity but it was not her place to do so. Sir Humphrey would prefer to do that himself, being the man he was, and it was none of her business.

'It promises to be a most unusual evening. The grandiose Martin. The close-lipped and uncommunicative Inspector. Mrs Rutherford. Master R. And why ever an Inspector? Perhaps the Youngs have been taking sheep or cattle. Reiving, after all these years! Imagine!'

'Imagine,' Abigail said and returned Ruskin to the shelf under the window.

She was glad she had brought one special gown. It was the colour of the peacocks and against it her hair showed at its best. Sir Humphrey's lady had arrived not long since but as Abigail was at that moment sitting in a painted hip-bath, deliciously replenished by hot water from copper cans, there was no opportunity of a preview from the window.

The gong boomed, the sound spreading like ripples on a pool then becoming faint and ghostly. Doors opened and closed. 'Abby?' Charity's voice impinged upon her soul-searching.

'Coming.'

The house had returned to life since Abigail's advent. The whole place creaked and stirred, snatches of conversation filtered from every direction. She was reminded of the low voices that had seemed to proceed from the locked Peacock Room. Only Charity had proved her wrong. The key. Who kept the key to the bed-chamber? Sir Humphrey, perhaps. But he had seemed surprised to find them there and had insisted upon remaining to lock the room himself.

Warmth and light flowed from the long, high-ceilinged dining-room. The rich flock paper, partially obscured by Scott portraits, vied with the gilded fresco for attention. A chandelier hung suspended on long chains of crystals. There were red candles in the branched silver-sticks, red roses in a corner, a dull red carpet patterned with golden flowers and sprawling leaves. The glasses and goblets were very fine, rivalling the chandelier for brilliance. A fire burned at either end of the room and a french window stood open so that the chamber would not become overheated. Through it, Abigail could see a purple sky set with stars and a thin sliver of moon.

Sir Humphrey stood by the head of the table, directly under the portrait of a blonde ancestor, and by his side was a woman who could only be the much-discussed Mrs Rutherford. She was not tall – Scott seemed to prefer small women – but there was no trace in her of Hope who resembled Johanne so greatly. Everything about Mrs Rutherford was clear-cut: her speaking voice, her shapely nose, the chiselled lips with the attractively blunted ends, the blue-whites of her magnificent eyes, the perfection of her hands and feet, the well-proportioned body. Not a hair of the neat, smooth style dared escape. Little she may be, but a force and a strength of will exuded from her, pervading and overcoming the despotism of the room.

The young man by the french window must be Mr Rutherford, Abigail calculated. He turned as Sir Humphrey greeted herself and Charity, revealing a pale, young face, as shuttered as Mrs Rutherford's was dynamic, proclaiming passion and self-will. His grey coat and light breeches did nothing to make him more dashing.

'So this is Miss Menory,' Mrs Rutherford said with more than a trace of crystal in her voice. The faceted hardness was not attractive to Abigail though Sir Humphrey seemed enthralled by it, listening closely to each utterance as to the oracle. 'I must confess I had expected someone – different.'

'Oh?' Abigail was nettled. 'How – different?'

'More like Charity.'

'Women are not made in moulds.'

'Women?' Mrs Rutherford gave a peal of laughter. 'I do not mock you, my dear, so put away that fierce expression, do. But you are still children, not all that long out of finishing school. And all wanting to grow up far too quickly.'

'I should call her eminently womanly,' a new voice put in quietly. 'It is not age that makes for maturity. I should say Miss Menory has been shaped by circumstance into a self-reliance she wears like a garment. Is that not so?'

Kenith Martin, long and feline, impeccably dressed in dark suit and white shirt that emphasized his Carolean appearance, was watching the scene from the doorway.

Abigail, a little annoyed, said, 'It is true I am made my own mistress because of the deaths of my only relatives. I had not thought it showed so plainly.'

'It always shows.'

'Are you saying,' Charity asked, 'that Abby appears advanced and I am backward? I being in the fortunate position of having most of my family around me? I can assure you it doesn't always follow – '

'Of course, I am not,' Martin answered, his smile maddening. 'It is a feminine trait to adopt almost any observation in the personal as opposed to the abstract. In other words I am saying that your reaction is another facet of womanhood. A very common one, at that.'

'And I,' Abigail was forced to comment, 'think that the remark was typical of the male. A trace of condescension we may well do without.' She could not understand her own prickliness.

'My dears!' Mrs Rutherford thrust out expressive hands. 'I appear to have stirred up a hornets' nest and quite unwittingly. I have not the pleasure of an introduction—'

'This is Mr Kenith Martin who is to photograph the house and everything in it,' Sir Humphrey explained with a hard look at Charity. She ought to be more careful, Abigail thought, then found Mr Martin's black eyes assessing her peacock-blue gown and a stray curl that had detached itself to twist upon her neck. For a moment she was terribly aware of that unwinking regard.

'Photograph the house? And all your treasures?' Some of the cadence seemed lacking from Mrs Rutherford's tones.

'It is the fashion,' Scott said carelessly. 'But also good sense. Where there is a recorded picture, a thing may not disappear without arousing comment.'

'Are you saying—?' Mrs Rutherford's eyes gleamed. Her son's eyes flickered and were dull again.

'Eleanor, I am saying nothing. Mr Martin—earlier, I admit, than I had planned—has arrived to make a painstaking inventory. He is so wrapped up in his work that he is unaware of the date. So, here he is.'

There was a subtle bristling of the Pringles around the room, waiting for the diners to be seated before they began the procession of serving and pouring, their minds absorbing this unwelcome news.

'Ah, Faith! I wondered where you were. Surely it is discourteous to be so tardy with so many guests?' Sir Humphrey showed definite displeasure with his sister, though there was no such condemnation of Hope who had come in with her aunt. For Hope there was only an uncharacteristic look of gentleness he showed no one else. 'And Geoffrey. Last, I see. It is time you met Peter Rutherford, Eleanor's son. Down from Edinburgh where he studied medicine. Seeking a practice.'

'How do you do,' Geoffrey growled uncomfortably, not reassured by a suddenly contemptuous glance from Rutherford. Some of Faith's angry colour began to subside into an unhappy pallor. Mrs Rutherford laid a possessive hand on one of the handsome pieces of *famille-rose* that graced the long table and it was plain Faith saw the writing on the wall.

'It cannot be real,' Eleanor breathed.

'It *is* real,' Scott asserted and, as if by accident, his hand brushed hers.

Abigail caught sight of Hope whose face was briefly transformed into a mask of utter detestation, a fact that did not go by unnoticed by Kenith Martin. Green eyes and black were caught in one reaction. Abigail's were first to look away but she took with her a sense of dark power, a penetration that was a warning.

'Mr Geoffrey is not last,' Martin said. 'We seem to have mislaid the Inspector.'

'Inspector?' Eleanor Rutherford's voice had risen an octave. 'Of – police?'

'An acquaintance,' Sir Humphrey answered. 'Hod. Will you find Inspector Moray? The rest of us will be seated. Peter, will you sit next to Hope? Mr Martin, on the left of Miss Menory, if you will – '

'Oh, I will.' Martin sounded pleased.

'And Geoff to the right.'

The Inspector, formal now in conservative suit, his

sandy hair slicked down, beard brushed and pomaded, came in red-faced and perspiring. Mrs Rutherford favoured him with a penetrating look.

'This, my dear, is Inspector Moray who will take his place beside you.'

'Sorry,' Moray said gruffly. 'Lost my way in the maze of passages.'

Again Eleanor Rutherford pealed with laughter. 'But how amusing! A policeman who has no sense of direction. Does that not make your job a difficult one?'

Some of Hope Scott's dislike infused Moray's answering stare. 'I am reasonably proficient at my own vocation,' he answered and sat down beside the widow who had shown such an unfortunate tendency to get on the wrong side of those she met.

The Pringles advanced, as though on a sortie, to pour soup and Eleanor, who had been stroking the edge of one of the *famille-rose* plates, narrowly escaped having her strong little fingers burnt. She gasped as the hot liquid sprayed and spotted the back of her hand and Sir Humphrey, furious, shouted, 'Can't you be careful! I can have you replaced!'

'My dear,' Eleanor said. 'I did tell you it was a mistake to maintain loyalty in such proportions over the years. If I were mistress here, I should have a *very* clean sweep.'

There was a terrible silence as all those busy hands were momentarily stilled and the ten members of the dinner party were favoured with inimical stares from Pringles of all shapes and sizes.

'Carry on,' Scott said awkwardly, obviously regretting his outburst. 'I spoke in the heat of the moment –'

'I did not,' Mrs Rutherford said, her brilliant eyes angry. 'Advantage can be taken and obviously is. You are too forgiving, Humphrey. But then that is your nature, is it not? Severity with fairness. A Christian spirit? But no unnecessary softness.'

'I like to think so.' Scott coloured with gratification and avoided Hod's grim scowl.

'But woe to the transgressor,' Charity could not resist saying, and Abigail saw Peter's eyes lift suddenly in perfect understanding. What did he know of Sir Humphrey?

Again Charity was impaled on a sharp look from her father and Abigail saw his lips form some biting retort. She spoke quickly. 'I saw an interesting building from the road today. A peel, I believe you call it, though in England it would be a tower or a keep. You said it was the Hanging Tower, didn't you, Charity?'

It was a pity Charity could not marry some congenial suitor and leave Duncraw, Abigail thought. If she were forced to stay here, to marry Geoffrey, she could one day be pushed over the edge of despair. A life wasted –

'Yes,' Charity said, careful again, reminded of her disobedience.

'Is there a history, Sir Humphrey?'

'Aye, there's a history. It's where a Crichton was once hanged. That's Cauldshiel land,' Sir Humphrey's voice was grudging, 'or so says the law. It was ours once. Then the burn changed its course; some quirk of nature; and since it was previously the boundary the Crichtons took what was left by the unexpected diversion. Refused to give it up.'

'So the Scotts hanged a man because of it?'

'The records say so,' Sir Humphrey said and yawned. 'I was not consulted.' He gave a bellow of laughter in which no one joined. 'It was a hundred years ago and more.'

'But say you *had* been there,' Peter Rutherford said. 'Would you have tied the rope?'

'If I thought the occasion warranted it, I suppose I might. I am a soldier and that training never deserts one. An officer can show no leniency towards disobedience and, if a position is taken, it must be reclaimed. That is how I should have viewed the hanging at the peel. Discipline. That's my vocation –'

'But what of human nature? Human frailties?' Peter persisted.

'In the army, you mean?'

'Since we are on military topics – But as a doctor I hold human life sacred –'

'I thought we were talking about the illegal possession of a piece of land,' Scott said, 'but since you ask my opinion, I've no time for weakness.'

'You've always been strong,' Eleanor Rutherford said, frowning at her son, her fingers laid intimately on Scott's arm as though to keep him in his seat. He relaxed.

'But how do you reconcile what could sound like vengefulness with the Christian beliefs I am assured you have?' Kenith Martin asked, one indolent hand resting on the white cloth.

Scott lifted his head and stared down the length of the table. 'The Bible advocates an eye for an eye. A tooth for a tooth.'

'So you act by the letter of the law,' Martin murmured, challenging his host. 'Everything clear cut.'

'Of course.'

'Then if one of your soldiers had some crisis at home, an unfaithful wife, or a dying child, and he was due to embark on an extended sojourn abroad, you could not forgive him for remaining at home to sort out the mess? If there was no one else?'

'He knew the regulations, the law that governs his taking of the Queen's shilling, the fact that he is no longer master of his own destiny. Anything else must take its own course.'

'But if his wife is lost to him, if the child dies?'

'Fortunes of war.' Sir Humphrey, who had succeeded in finishing his soup in spite of the interrogation, shrugged and remained handsomely unmoved.

'That does not seem Christ's way,' Charity said.

'I spoke of God.'

'But are they not the same?' Kenith Martin interposed.

'I have never seen it that way,' Scott told him. 'I find Father and Son are poles apart. The Father I understand and that is why I read the Old Testament. It's more a soldier's account.'

'Less forgiving, of course,' Eleanor Rutherford commented, 'but a great soldier can be expected to prefer battles and a God of war and vengeance. Personally, I have had enough of gloom for one evening. Your dinners are usually so much more amusing, my dear,' this with one of her diamond-hard looks at Scott and a showing of a dimple in her left cheek, that passed for a smile.

Abigail alone saw Hod's glance of controlled dislike, Hope's pale resentment before she lowered her brown eyes to a plate newly heaped with roast fowl and its attendant vegetables.

'We have heard nothing of your distinguished career.' Kenith Martin took up the conversation which had flagged during the Pringles' industrious foray round the table. 'When you projected the plan to make a detailed record of Duncraw, its books and furnishings, I took the liberty of researching your military past and found its outline interesting. It could be even more so were there more flesh on the bones. Were you not at Sebastopol?'

Scott frowned. 'Aye. I was there. And at Balaclava.

But I'd prefer not to go into that this evening. Sieges and battles are men's work and of little interest to the opposite sex but to promote whimpers of distress and dismay. Since we are in the presence of so many ladies, I suggest we keep that for the smoking-room or the port. I confess I'm as interested in the history of the camera and that surely could not provoke feminine cries of "Enough." Eleanor would prefer to be entertained. What about you, Miss Menory?'

'I should be enthralled,' Abigail said, hoping no one would detect the note of irony. She had imagined earlier that Martin would be easy to like because of his picturesque flamboyance, the Stuart charm, but he had depths that concealed the real man. Even Peter Rutherford was not the dullard he first appeared. Charity had changed – or worse – had been changed, and Hope was unlikely ever to speak a word unless directly addressed. Faith was eaten up with jealousy over the treasures of Duncraw being touched, and not so unlikely, being owned eventually by Mrs Rutherford who still caressed the *famille-rose* in spite of the episode of the splashed soup; Geoffrey jealous too, but because of Charity's indifference. The Inspector attended to his food with the obvious wish to remain as unobtrusive as possible, as though his approaching need to probe into so many sensitive areas oppressed him. All of them with their own particular and not always pleasant axe to grind. It was far removed from the excitement of the unfolding Border country, but the encounter with the gipsy, who promised nothing but shadows and difficulties, seemed already to bear fruit.

'You, Miss Menory, would be an excellent subject,' Martin was saying, 'except that it would be a pity your colouring would be lost. You have an enviable stillness. Most people are too volatile or too nervous. One gets a forced expression and then one is compelled to live with a portrait of a relative who can do nothing but glare down from the wall like a pole-axed bull – or an incipient murderess.'

Abigail laughed suddenly. He painted an amusing picture. Life came back into Martin's black eyes. The long face resumed its aspect of mischief. 'That is much better,' he murmured so that only she heard. 'Now you look alive.'

'It is often said photography is an unnecessary invention and takes the bread from the mouths of artists,' Mrs Rutherford said, determined dimples much in evidence.

Martin looked at her for a moment. 'There is surely room for both?' His tone was cool.

'I have a cousin who is quite penurious as a result.'

'Mother,' Peter ventured uncomfortably. 'May it not be more truthful that her workmanship is not good? I find her water-colours insipid. They did not sell *before* lithographs and such-like.'

'Peter is such an *honest* young man,' Eleanor Rutherford pronounced and the glint in her magnificent eyes boded ill for her son when they were alone. 'And now, Humphrey, my dear, we seem to have finished the meal. Adequate, though I should have used rosemary, and the gravy did tend to be lumpy. Still, I suppose with your obvious staffing problems, there are bound to be areas of disappointment. A new broom is what you need – long overdue!'

Abigail listened, every nerve expecting the flight of some Pringle halberk or deer-knife in the direction of the tiny Amazon but the hairy hands went on lifting and piling, carrying trays and opening doors as though she did not exist.

'You said you would show us the *pièce de résistance*,'

Eleanor went on serenely, dabbing her pretty lips with her napkin. 'The Peacock Room – '

She never finished the sentence for there was a splintering crash and something lay in fragments on the floor. A piece of the priceless *famille-rose*.

THREE

Sir Humphrey sprang to his feet. Eleanor Rutherford gave a faintly metallic scream. 'Oh, that beautiful plate!'

'That *expensive* plate,' Kenith Martin murmured.

'How could you!' Abigail whispered.

'I was testing you. I'm glad you have a soul.'

'I picked it up. My hand shook and it fell.' Hope did not apologize, only stood there looking at the patterned pieces as though her thoughts were far removed.

Scott harrumphed awkwardly. 'I cannot say I am pleased –'

'If I had done it you'd have said enough!' Charity cried. 'Or if it had been Jeannie or one of them.' She stopped, seeing her father's anger.

Mrs Rutherford gave a small, distressed cry and fell to her knees on the red and gold carpet. 'See, Humphrey! It may not be entirely lost. The breaks are clean. Take no notice of Charity. She's upset, as we all are. I'm certain Hope did not intend the mishap.' Her small, strong hand pulled at Scott's sleeve, forcing him to examine the portions of the plate with her.

But Hope had intended the vandalism. It was written all over her brown, remote face. The enemy of Duncraw had touched and coveted the china so Hope had destroyed it.

'It can be mended,' Eleanor pronounced, 'though it

will never have the same appearance or value. But it could have been worse – '

'May I go to my room, Father?' Hope asked, moving before he had had time to reply.

'There is no need. An accident – ' He shrugged as though it were a small matter.

She turned and gave him a brief, scornful smile he must have understood. Or did he see only what he wanted to? Abigail thought this must be so, for he put his arm through Mrs Rutherford's and said heartily, 'I promised everyone a treat this evening. A tour of the house. Martin must see it because of those all-important pictures. The Inspector has his appetite whetted by mutual acquaintances. Young Rutherford has not been here before and there must be corners Miss Menory has missed.'

'I'm sure there are.'

'So stay, Hope. You see there was an announcement I was to make just at the moment you – er – broke the dish – '

'Announcement?' Hope's eyes were enormous yet quite without depth.

'I see you may have guessed. That is why Peter is here. Eleanor has consented, at last, to be my wife. I have – er – laid siege to her for near as long as it took to relieve Sebastopol and the outcome is as happy. And it is not the only announcement I am pleased to say. Geoffrey has asked my consent to marry my daughter, Charity, and I am delighted to say I approve. So this is a double celebration. Stay, Hod, all of you, and drink to both prospective brides.'

Abigail hardly dared to look at her friend. What she saw surprised her. Though pale, Charity did not seem surprised or even unduly perturbed. Geoffrey moved to her side as though he could not believe the evidence of his ears. Faith's expression was a mixture of hostility towards Eleanor and of an uneasy relief that Charity was, after all, to become her daughter-in-law. Life could be extremely uncomfortable with a new mistress in the place, but there was the future to plan for – look forward to.

Hope had not waited for the toasts to be drunk. Eleanor noticed her departure and said, 'The child is bound to need time to adjust. She's had you to herself for long enough. I dare say Peter would have felt the same at her age – '

'You lost your husband when?' Faith asked, raising a glass, two hard spots of colour high in her cheeks.

'During the Crimea,' Eleanor answered and turned away as though she wished not to continue the topic. It had been tactless of Faith to refer to her previous marriage.

A spate of disjointed and uneasy conversation broke out, during which the Pringles sipped a token toast which might well have been hemlock considering the aspect of gloom that lowered over the hirsute faces, then carried on with the clearing of the table.

Kenith Martin, his glass still half-full, moved purposefully in front of Abigail. 'What think you of the household?' he enquired very softly, his dark gaze hooded. 'It smacks to me of Greek tragedies and Stygian rivers. Little suggestion of family loyalties and where they do exist they are – '

'Morbid or vitiated?'

'Exactly, Miss Menory.'

'But that need not concern you, Mr. Martin – '

'Kenith.'

'You are merely here to take your pictures. The rest – ' She shrugged. 'That is not in our hands. We shall be allowed to watch you at work?'

'Well – now and again,' he conceded. 'I find myself intimidated by too much scrutiny.'

She laughed with real amusement. 'You? If ever anyone enjoyed an audience it is you, Mr Martin –'

'Kenith.'

'Kenith –'

'And I may call you Abigail? It has a peculiar fitness. A John Knox directness allied to a smatter of imagination. A spirited name with the right dash of romanticism –'

'There's little romantic about me, Mr – Kenith. You must set your sights elsewhere if that is what you are looking for.'

'Everyone else is suddenly spoken for. Mrs R. Your friend, Charity. Hope is too young, even if I cared for changelings. And there is something about a moustached woman that saps my virility.'

Abigail could not restrain a smile. 'You are unkind. Did you really meet the Inspector at the foot of the drive when you arrived?'

'Of course.' The deep eyelids were raised to show her dark shrewdness. 'Why should I lie?'

'He – seemed to know you better at one point in the dinner talk. Only I no longer remember the place. It was almost as if he reproved you.'

'I am afraid he disapproves instantly as so many do. I am considered neither businessman nor craftsman. I merely steal likenesses like a thief. To take a counterpart is to steal the soul. On occasion I have even been accused of being the Devil –'

'Oh, how lovely!' Abigail raised her glass. 'I wish I had been there.'

'And Abby has been the cause of keeping the pilchard boats in harbour because the crew saw her first thing in the morning and she has red hair,' Charity said, appearing unexpectedly by Kenith's shoulder.

'So,' he said gravely. 'We are both suspect. Both necromancers. I had not realized this was to be your betrothal, Miss Scott. May I offer my congratulations?'

'You are not the only one to be surprised. But, thank you.'

'Surely you had some idea?'

'Oh, yes. But I convinced myself – Oh, don't let's harp on it. I do believe we are about to begin the grand tour. I see the Master and Mistress of Ceremonies at the door. I simply must have another glass of champagne. Would you – ? Oh, thank you, Hod. Yes, we will all have more. Do not argue, Abby. We require fortifying. You against the blandishments of Mr Martin. I against – ' Charity turned away quickly and began to circumvent the long table, her steps stumbling.

Mrs Rutherford's voice floated back with devastating clarity. 'But I thought it was the approved thing. For brides to sleep in the Peacock Room. In the Peacock Bed.'

There was a silence, then Sir Humphrey said, 'But really, Eleanor. That was long ago. No one's done it since – '

'Felicity Croser?' Charity suggested.

'Not since then. Or not that I heard of.'

'I should like to.' The thin steel was back in Eleanor's voice. 'It's – a challenge.'

'But it would have to be aired for at least a week. Probably more – '

'I'm quite content to wait. But you wouldn't deny me a small wish like that, would you, my dear?'

'No. Of course not. I was only – caught off guard.'

'And you a soldier?' Mrs Rutherford's laughter rang out. 'That's not tactics, is it?'

'You are teasing me.' Scott's tones were fond.

'Of course. I was afraid you would take evasive measures – '

73

'You are doing it again. All this military talk.'

They laughed together.

Abigail caught sight of Charity's scornful pallor. The pain in her eyes was more than she could bear. 'Oh, my poor Charity –'

'I am afraid you are right,' Kenith Martin murmured. 'Must she be compelled?'

'She must,' Abigail said quietly and bitterly. 'An old grudge –'

'You must tell me –'

She faced him, her skin very white against the glowing hair. 'Why must I? A man who will be here for a week or so while he tries to preserve the laird's materialistic treasures? At the moment I could set fire to them all with pleasure. Or kill him –'

'He is not – lovable.'

'I thought I liked him when I came. But I see I was wrong. He and that woman are laying up more trouble between them than anyone will be able to cope with –'

'For someone who was going to preserve a discreet silence, you have a great deal to say. Though I'd prefer the specific. I have an unfortunate and unbecoming curiosity –'

'Unfortunate! Curiosity! I'll not be your microscope.'

Martin laughed delightedly. 'Dash as well as soul. Why are we not celebrating your engagement this evening?'

'You are impertinent.' Abigail, aware that they lagged behind the rest, hastened to catch up with the party. Martin caught at her wrist.

'No. Let us follow at a safe distance. They will all be occupied with their uncomfortable war games. Mrs R. playing on the feelings of Scott's daughters; threatening the family retainers. By God! She's braver than

Napoleon. He plays with fire by this projected alliance. Both girls dead set against it. Sister Faith seething. Nephew divided between triumph and despair. And I saw Peter Rutherford look at Scott with detestation when no one else observed – '

'Quite the student of human behavior – ' She detached her hand from his.

'It is part of my work. An important part if I am to bring subjects to life – '

'But your subjects are inanimate. Books and porcelain. Tapestries and silver.'

'Only you *will* allow me to photograph you? I find suddenly I don't care about the rest.'

'I don't know,' she whispered, aware that this man excited her by his proximity, his own brand of elegance. He was not handsome. But there was that charm that came – and went, as suddenly. She was not so foolish as to miss the occasional hardness, the near ruthlessness. Apart from Colin Crichton, Kenith Martin was the only man in the neighbourhood she could imagine pulling a woman on the saddle of his horse and galloping into the murky Border night. A shiver of almost pleasurable danger ran the length of her spine.

She hurried up the stairs, aware of the sound of his following steps, then she stopped abruptly. From the window she saw the lights from downstairs shine on a mounted figure beyond the lawn. It was a man in a grey coat and something about the set of his head reminded her of Colin. He waved. At her?

There was a distant shout, the sharp crack of a shot, then the horse and rider vanished behind the lines of trees.

'What is it?' Martin asked, pressing his face close to the glass.

'I – saw nothing. It may be an intruder. The Pringles have their own laws. As do the Youngs –'

'Youngs?'

'The personal servants of the Crichtons of whom you've already heard. I was stopped by one of them – armed – this morning –'

'On Scott territory?'

'No. Well, if you must know, it was at the Hanging Tower.'

'So you did *not* stay on the road.'

'I did not want to incur Sir Humphrey's displeasure by admitting it. But it was unintentional –'

'May I ask how you got out of the predicament?'

'Young Mr Crichton came and sent his man packing.'

'Then there really is still bad blood between the families?'

'Quite definitely.'

'Troubles both internal and external. Thefts. It cannot be what you envisaged when you were invited.'

'No, Mr Martin, none of it is as I imagined. But I had a warning – of sorts.'

'How? A letter?' He sounded excited.

'A gipsy on the road a mile from Duncraw. I must beware shadows and men in grey. It's all nonsense, of course.'

'I have a grey cape. Peter Rutherford a grey coat. I dare say Sir Humphrey has some garment in that colour –'

But Abigail was no longer aware of the noise of people running past them to the ground floor, of Sir Humphrey's shouted orders. She was thinking of Crichton with his curly hair and handsome face, of the man who had crossed the hill beyond the Scott burial-ground last night. Somewhere in this plethora of grey could lurk the subject of the old woman's prediction. She swung around but Martin was no longer there.

Sir Humphrey appeared at breakfast later than usual. Abigail wondered where he had spent the night and then was vaguely shocked by her own thoughts. But Mrs Rutherford had expressed her determination to sleep in the beautiful Yellow Room since the Peacock Bed was still out of bounds and there had been opening and closing of doors – very softly – for some time last night.

Abigail told herself she was becoming one of the dreaded prying spinsters and made a mental resolve to take a cold bath, but the arrival of Kenith Martin distracted her from the unseemly conjecturing. His presence lightened the atmosphere immediately. It was, she realized, one of his charming periods. She watched him covertly, lifting the silver covers on the sideboard, choosing his food with great delicacy.

He sat down, eyeing the crisped bacon and solitary egg with a pleasure Sir Humphrey had not had in his own frugal and business-like breakfast. His army ways had not left him. He still behaved as though entitled only to iron rations.

Charity slid, pale and quiet, into her seat.

'You must begin to think of some clothes,' Scott told her without preamble. 'You should go to Peebles or Galashiels for materials and Faith will accompany you. She'd enjoy fitting out a bride. She's always bemoaned the fact she's no daughter – '

'I should prefer Abigail's company.'

Encouraged by the fact that his difficult Charity had not refused outright to begin the preparations for the marriage arranged for her, Scott said, 'Well, Geoffrey ought to ride with you.'

'Must he?' Charity asked wearily.

'You must become used to his perpetual presence,' Scott reminded her quietly.

Perpetual presence! Had he used the watchdog expression purposely, Abigail wondered hotly, then found Kenith's expressive gaze on hers. It seemed he agreed with her.

'We could perhaps take the carriage,' Abigail suggested. 'The coachman would be chaperon enough. Men are notoriously disinterested in feminine shopping. Then, if there are purchases, we'd have somewhere to stow them.'

Scott grunted noncommittally. 'How else would you go shopping? Of course you must take the carriage.'

'I dare say you have your own plan of campaign for today?' Abigail suggested, seeing Martin was not eating at that moment.

'I'll be very much in everyone's way, I fear. I can leave the van in the coachhouse, Sir Humphrey? I have to set up my dark room and the van would be best where it is.'

'Naturally. If that should prove unsuccessful, there are cellars below.'

'Capital. No sign of last night's intruder?'

'None at all.' A spark of anger flared in Scott's blue gaze.

Abigail lowered her eyes, glad of the advent of Inspector Moray who surveyed the dishes on the sideboard more as if they were works of art than intended to be utilitarian.

'Fine silver,' he commented, lifting a plate and fork. He should be an authority.

'Queen Anne,' Scott told him. 'You may go where you will, both of you. The servants have been told their rooms may be examined. My daughters also.'

'We may as well go, Abby,' Charity said, rising. She had eaten scarcely anything. 'I thought you would want to see as much as you can while it is fine. And Mr Martin says we will only be in his way.'

'Not so bluntly, I hope,' Kenith protested amiably, dabbing at his lips with a very white napkin.

'What Mr Martin said was that *he* would be in the way,' Scott observed with dislike. 'How long will you be away, Charity?' His tone suggested it could be forever for all he'd care.

'All day. We can have luncheon wherever we happen to be when we feel hungry.'

The two girls retired upstairs to put on their bonnets and fetch sunshades for the day promised to be hot. When Abigail came out of her bed-chamber, she found Charity ready, a letter held in one hand.

'Will you post it in Peebles?' she asked, but her friend seemed not to have heard.

'Hm?' Charity murmured. 'I'm sure they will have nothing of fashion. I may have to go to Edinburgh eventually. The carriage is ready. I saw it from the window.'

It was a beautiful morning, the yews black as ink, the sunlight bouncing off the pink marble with its mossy creases and off the glass panes of the windows. Impossible to see whether their departure was noticed but the Pringles would know.

They set off in the direction of the Hanging Tower and, as they approached it, Abigail saw it with new eyes, saw the temporary gibbet, the dangling corpse, its neck horribly awry, legs swinging idly. Or had they pushed him from one of the windows to choke and claw at the gritty wall? It would have been less troublesome and just as effective. She shivered. She had had no such thoughts before she came to Duncraw, yet now they emanated from the earth and the river, from the rough stones that once housed the enemies of yesterday, stronger than anything she had ever known.

They had just drawn level with the stepping-stones when Charity leaned from the window and threw something towards the base of the peel. Abigail saw it lie there in the clump of nettles, a portion of white, caught and held by the jagged leaves. The letter.

'Charity – '

'I have to tell him. He'll come some time this morning – '

'Did you know he was at Duncraw last night? I saw him by the trees.'

'No. That was foolish. He might have been shot. Dead, even – ' The girl's hands shook.

'You wrote of your engagement to Geoffrey?'

'Yes. And that it was not my wish. But he knows that already.'

'That was all? No – foolishness?'

'My letter is my own affair, Abby.'

'Of course. It's – I am on your side.'

'I should not have written to you, subjecting you to all that's happened. But it seemed like any other summer...'

'Forget it for the present. See how the wild flowers thrust up through the strong grass. And the hills are more brown than green. Goblin hills. And the sheep are singing – '

Charity burst out laughing. 'Sheep do not sing!'

'All on one note, or is it two? As though they had pegs on their noses.'

'No wonder Mr Martin shows an interest in you, Abby. You are original.'

'Does he?' Abigail was surprised that Charity noticed anything but her own misery.

'You know he does. A pity he seems such a dilettante. Do you suppose a photographer can afford to keep a wife?'

'He may have money of his own and this a mere hobby.'

'You'd like to know, wouldn't you? But be careful, Abby, dear. There's a cold look about him at times as if we were all in some dissecting chamber and he deciding which of us to start on.'

'Charity, it's too good a day for pessimism. Let tomorrow look after itself.' Abigail set herself to enjoy the glitter of the sun on the stream, the warm sweet smell of the honeysuckle in the hedge. But she was free and Charity in bondage. The pleasure did not come. She put out her hand and took Charity's. 'It may never happen – '

'It *will* never happen. I'll see to that.'

'Well, now that's decided, is that a pheasant I see in the field?'

'Yes. And if you look on the wall there, you'll see a rather young and extrovert weasel dancing on the tumbled stone.'

Abigail gave an excited cry. There was so much that was new and interesting. What a pity it must be spoiled by undercurrents.

Charity, who was leaning out of the other window, suddenly sat very upright against the back of the coach. Her pale cheeks were now faintly flushed with colour. Abigail could not fathom the change in her, then returned to the contemplation of the wild, winding road and the brown river sewn with spangles, the floating background of larch and birch, of pine and beech, the glimpses of ruin, the sharp whiteness of a farm or cottage, the eternal sheep and their folds, the crows that perched and jeered like ragged men at a bad play.

Peebles was set in a bowl of hills, a small grey town

where the carriage springs were sorely tried on the cobbles and the meagre shops given over to wool and tartans and very little in the way of bridal materials. Charity seemed in no way put out, emerging from the last shop.

'We'll go to Hawick, then,' she said.

'I could ride all day and never tire of your Border,' Abigail agreed, climbing back inside the coach and watching the shadows of leaves and chimney pots on the rounded cobbles.

They went by Innerleithen and Walkerburn, seeing a fair house in the distance that Charity called Traquair, but when the carriage approached Selkirk, Abigail was visited by a sudden and compelling sadness she could not explain.

'It's an ill place,' she said to her disgust when Charity suggested lunching there. 'I can feel it in my bones. It has a taste of – death.'

'It's the place where the Duke of Montrose was defeated. See down there on the flat ground by the meeting of the waters?'

Charity took a firm hold of her reticule as it slipped sideways from her lap. It seemed inordinately heavy.

'Have you brought a hoard of sovereigns with you?' Abigail asked, joking, but Charity looked displeased and drew away.

'We will wait till we reach Hawick for luncheon, I think.'

'Very well. I am not hungry,' Abigail agreed and wondered what she had said to offend.

By the time Hawick was reached, the coachman was perspiring and red of face, easily persuaded to go into the tap-room of the Lamb and Flag while the girls toyed with a meal in the dining-room of the hotel.

'I think,' Charity said, 'I require the ladies' room. Would you keep my place for me?'

'Of course.'

It was quiet in the dark room after she had gone. The lacy parasol looked gay and pretty against the heavy, Victorian furniture as though Charity had left the ghost of herself.

Two dark-suited gentlemen seated themselves at the next table and ordered lamb chops and cabinet pudding. They discussed wool sales for a few minutes while Abigail wondered what could be keeping Charity.

'Saw Crichton just before I met you,' the stouter man volunteered.

'Young Colin? He usually calls when he is in Hawick. But they've troubles enough at Cauldshiel and he probably shrinks from spreading gloom.

'The fabric of the house is deteriorating and only the last high winds revealed the state of the roof. His much-vaunted horse has not won a single race this season and there's been disease in the cattle. He's hard-pressed to lay his hands on money, poor lad. The father's worse than an invalid, I hear, and the worries rest on Colin's shoulders.'

'I do not envy him, then. Not much left but the old resort, eh? A lass with moneybags and not much else to recommend her. It's the age-old way out of the difficulty.' The speaker frowned as though this had been the way he himself found his entry into matrimony.

'Not necessarily the case with Crichton. If I'm not mistaken –' the man craned his neck to see the better out of the small window, 'that's Scott's young filly he's guiding round the back of the fountain. Now there's prospective fortune without the usual bitter pill."

'I thought they were at daggers drawn, Colin and Humphrey?'

'Then either Scott has relented or we are witnessing

an illicit meeting. I can't blame Crichton. A fetching little thing. Wish I were twenty years younger.'

Abigail got up and went to look for herself. Sure enough, Charity and Crichton were standing by the fountain which looked as though fashioned from brawn set with green taps, and the girl was in the process of handing him a parcel from the interior of the white reticule. It was wrapped in linen as though to preserve it and was shaped like a small statuette or a vase. Too heavy for a vase, Abigail remembered, thinking of the joke that had fallen flat. Thinking too of the overheard conversation, she had a sudden sick conviction that she knew who was responsible for the loss of Sir Humphrey's valuables.

She watched Colin Crichton smile, the sun glint on the brown, shiny curls. The quick pressure of an arm round Charity's lilac-clad waist, the touch of white fingers and brown, a pause, then a most indiscreet embrace that must have been noticed by most of the midday promenaders and shoppers. They looked just like Shakespeare's ill-fated lovers, she thought emptily. A fair, fragile Juliet, a sunburnt Romeo with Botticelli curls. All they needed was the white-foot nag of the old Border ballad.

The sunlight in the square seemed to shiver into fragments. Crichton had gone, lost behind the ridiculous marble of the fountain, and Charity, light as air, her eyes seeing into some unknown dimension, sped towards the hotel door, her pale skirts floating.

It was all quite clear. The thrown letter. The moment when Charity had seen Colin following. The excuse to leave the dining-room. Abigail could have forgiven a sweethearts' meeting. But for Crichton to encourage Charity to steal in order to pay his debts. That was shabby. She had not thought that of him and the realization was bitter.

Abigail, cold in spite of the warmth of the day, waited, her hand stroking the artless frivolity of the parasol, wishing she could bring back innocence.

Charity made a show of inspecting laces and muslins, bolts of creamy silk, but dismissed them all for the present. 'If I see nothing better elsewhere, I shall return here.'

She seemed unaware of Abigail's abstraction, her own thoughts occupied to capacity by the furtive meeting with Crichton. Not that it had been kept from everyone. Abigail remembered the embrace by the fountain and was assailed by emptiness. It was not as though she wanted Crichton for herself. Only that she wished someone wanted her sufficiently to throw caution to the winds, to proclaim their need of her. The only thing wrong with her was loneliness. There seemed no one who could not get along perfectly well without her.

The shadows grew long as the carriage approached Duncraw. Peebles was left behind, the hills had turned blue. The thin moon pirouetted like some dance-drunk naiad. Hod Pringle appeared in the drive, his fowling-piece business-like. Hod seemed in evidence everywhere. At table, in the grounds, drinking with the master late in the evening. But not for much longer. Once Eleanor was Lady Scott, and this she plainly intended, Hod would be given his *congé*.

The evening meal was quieter than usual. Faith kept herself in check though she was obviously disturbed, twisting her napkin, dropping a spoon or fork. Geoffrey confined himself to gazing at Charity, she quite oblivious of him, or of sharp looks from Scott. Eleanor, in a blue gown that showed up her magnificent eyes, smiled forgivingly at Hope, no doubt in the anticipation that she would break no more *famille-*

rose. Hope stared back unwinkingly. She was so unyoung, Abigail thought, her gaze flicking over the Inspector and noting the tidiness of hair and beard in comparison with his nervousness of the morning.

Kenith Martin was in his place beside her, dark and inscrutable as if he worked out some problem. He turned towards Abigail. 'Would you care to see my dark room, Miss Menory?' he asked quietly, under cover of the clatter of plates.

'What should I see?'

'Why, darkness, of course.'

'Then what is the point?'

'I did not think you obtuse.'

'Oh, I am not that.'

'Then come. It has been a dull day. The laird and his lady riding. Miss Hope in the graveyard – '

'Again?'

'Everyone else invisible but for the Inspector. Wherever I was, he was there also.'

'I should have thought he'd be mustering Pringles.'

'He must first count the books, see for himself the positions of each ornament or picture. You can have no idea of his fussiness.'

'A man like him cannot afford to gain a reputation for carelessness. And Sir Humphrey *is* a martinet. One must please one's employer.'

'What do you think of policemen?'

'I have never given them much thought. But the Inspector has an eye for objects of value.'

'So have I. I do not wish you to slip through my fingers like that piece of *famille-rose*. I want you on a sofa – '

'Mr Martin!'

'Oh, sitting bolt-upright. In black velvet with a low neckline, and touches of green – small bows perhaps.

And a rose. A rather unobtrusive rose. And that magnificent hair – '

'You – like it?'

'It's the most beautiful thing I have ever seen – '

'Isn't it true, Abigail, that the selection of materials we saw today was disappointing?' Charity's clear voice cut across their soft-tongued fencing.

'It was better in Hawick than anywhere else, but Edinburgh would be best.'

'We could go together,' Mrs Rutherford suggested, dimpling. 'I know I will not be able to wear white, but the city will provide so much choice. I could advise you, Charity. And Hope should accompany us. She should attend you.'

'I do not care for weddings,' Hope said too loudly. 'And I dislike dressing up. I'm sure Miss Menory would suit so much better than I.'

'Miss Menory may not be here. She is a passing guest,' Eleanor said rather sharply.

'I will not be at the weddings,' Hope maintained.

'But you must. I should feel that you objected in some way – '

'Then you would feel rightly.'

'Hope! You will go to your room. And you'll not appear at table until you have apologized,' her father expostulated angrily.

'Very well.' Hope rose quite calmly and walked from the room with great self-control.

'We shall have difficulties there, I fear,' Eleanor pointed out, possessive fingers on Scott's arm. 'Peter. Could you not try to win her over? It seems I cannot and she is bound to hold it against Charity for – er, for Johanne.'

A flicker of pain passed through Scott's eyes. He still reacted to her memory, just as her daughters did, Abigail saw. Johanne would always remain here at

Duncraw, her shadow over the pink marble, the peacock carving, over this dining-table, over the marital bed.

'I will speak to her if I am able –' Peter began unwillingly, 'though it's not my place –'

'No. I must do it,' Scott insisted. 'She's my problem. I've allowed her too much laxity. She seemed so small and forlorn –'

'And now she is strong and self-willed, has her own weapons, and you cannot find the proper strategy.' Eleanor smiled intimately as she played on the martial theme that had amused Scott last night but he did not respond. 'We will take the carriage tomorrow, love; and leave the place to fend for itself. You need a change. Things will sort themselves out.'

'Perhaps.'

'What was the book you mentioned specifically?' Inspector Moray asked, dabbing at his moustache. 'One of those missing?'

'It was an early book by the Bishop of Northumbria. *Philosophies and the Practical*. An olive-green binding. Gold-tooled. Illuminated capitals.'

'Ah, yes. I just wished to be clear, if you are likely to be unavailable tomorrow.' The Inspector took out a note-book. 'And there was the chinoiserie caddy, the Isaac Oliver miniature, the de Lamerie snuff-box, the Clichy paper-weight, the Waterford –'

'I should prefer it if we joined forces in my study after dinner?' Scott suggested, seeming taken aback by the Inspector's unexpected revelations over the sacred ceremony of food-taking. Or was it a cunning way of revealing his knowledge of what was taken?

'Well, there will be no need if I can just add the jade statuette. Six inches high. Grey-green. Chinese figure, arms folded – a fairly heavy piece.'

'That is correct,' Sir Humphrey said shortly.

Abigail sat perfectly still. The linen-wrapped parcel had been about so high, and she had noticed the weight of Charity's reticule. Before the Inspector had spoken, she had suspected the object to be that of a small statue. Charity had become alien to her and she no longer had a motive for remaining at Duncraw. A great longing overcame Abigail. She wanted to belong to someone, to be essential. To anyone –

'If the dark room does not appeal . . . then . . . the garden,' Kenith Martin suggested very softly. Very seductively. He had admired her detested and mistrusted hair. But he was undoubtedly an adventurer who had chosen a temporarily lucrative channel for his creativity.

'I have no dowry, Mr Martin. I feel obliged to warn you.' The wine with the meal had obviously gone to her head.

'I do not give a fig for the revelation. Money is sordid. Then you'll take a turn on the terrace?'

'I confess I long for fresh air – '

'Very well, then. As soon as it is practicable, we escape.'

Escape to what? An undignified fumble in the shrubbery? A venturesome hand and a slap to that rather ugly, yet altogether fascinating face? Abigail did not care. She would be free of other and more damaging antagonisms, shorn of the necessity of being agreeable to Charity who had so disappointed her. She did not blame her for loving Crichton, for inventing meetings with him; she did not really covet that brown, handsome head with the Bacchanalian curls and the open smile. She hated to be part of deceit and treachery.

The attendant Pringles became, inexplicably, more than part of the domestic background. Hod was there, sunburnt and spare, an integral part of Scott's past life. Everything he did was neat and soldierly. Something screamed terribly and the lean strong hand never wavered.

Eleanor gasped and looked towards the window, remembering the shots of last night.

'See that the birds are shut up,' Sir Humphrey ordered and helped himself from the decanter. It seemed he also required fortifying. 'It's only the peacocks.'

'Are you sure?'

'I should know by this time, my dear.' Scott did not seem so enamoured as previously. Perhaps the memories evoked by Hope's intransigence had been stronger than he expected. Hope and Johanne could still win.

The meal came to an end. The women, as expected, rose to go. Martin leaned across and whispered, 'By the yew at the end of the terrace. In half an hour.'

'Very well.'

As usual, the female members of the household separated. Here, there was no cosy gathering in another room. Eleanor swept off in the direction of the Yellow Chamber. Faith went towards Mrs Davison's room. Charity said, 'I think I would like to retire early, Abby. Would you mind awfully?'

'I should not mind at all.'

Charity seemed not to notice the brusqueness. Abigail left her abruptly and went to the french window that led to the terrace. Loneliness was a poor excuse for seeking the company of a man one did not trust. But he was not dull. The interlude would be entertaining enough, whatever the outcome.

Martin was waiting where he had said he would be. The great shadows of the yews slanted over the pavingstones. The moon was much clearer, thin and fragile as a bow. 'You look so different in the dark,' he said. 'Your vitality drowned. You should always be outlined in light. Come, stand in front of a window. That's better. I have thought of a place to take your portrait. On the Peacock Bed. The tail behind you like an enormous fan.'

'There may be objections.'

'No one need know.'

He smiled, and even in the darkness his teeth were white and perfect. She saw him in half-armour, astride a shire horse, a plume in his wide-brimmed hat. She knew it must have been a shire for nothing else could have carried a man encased in steel.

He reached out and pulled her close beside him. 'I discover I do not wish to see you go from Duncraw. I should miss that delightful intelligence and curiosity. You suffer from my besetting sin, do you not? I see it ignite every so often. Miss Charity has been up to some trick, I suspect. Did she – meet Mr Crichton?'

Abigail jerked away. 'What do you know of that?'

'The Pringles are not all averse to strangers.'

'I thought you could not reconcile yourself to moustached women?'

'Who mentioned women? Men have mouths.'

'I had noticed.'

'Yours is the kind I am tempted to kiss.'

The night was suddenly quiet, yet filled with urgency. It was an experiment only, Abigail told herself as he leaned towards her. But there was nothing tentative in the result. She had made up her mind to push him away but found that she could not, did not even want to. He was warm, strong and surprisingly seductive and there was no mistaking the fact that he was enjoying the experience. A sensual man – just like the Stuart.

Abigail woke with a sense of well-being. There was no sun but her body was bathed in warmth as though she were lying on a rug in front of a fire. Her mind struggled between dreams and reality, shutting out one kind of darkness, accepting another almost gratefully. Someone bent over her. 'Ken –' she began to say, then recognized Jeannie standing with the morning tea.

'Do I ken what, Miss Abigail?' The girl's expression was curious. 'You've adopted Scots words.'

'I've completely forgotten what I was going to say.' Abigail sat up and took the cup.

'It's a dour morning. But everyone's up that early. You'd think they had bad consciences.'

'Everyone?' She sipped pleasurably. Jeannie had remembered no milk and a slice of lemon.

'Aye. Madame Rutherford – beg pardon – Mrs Rutherford and the laird are away to Edinburgh, I think in half an hour. Miss Charity sent me to fetch you. She seems to need company. Mr Geoffrey's off to visit various friends.'

'Mr Martin – Inspector Moray? Are they – ?'

'I just met Mr Martin on the stair. A roguish gentleman. The Inspector is at breakfast.'

'I really must get up, then.' Abigail's eyes were bright. 'And you won't want Mrs Davison asking where you've been.'

'No, miss.'

Abigail had never washed so quickly. She chose a yellow dress and brushed her hair loose. It could be pinned up later. In five minutes she was in the dining-room. Sir Humphrey and Eleanor had gone and of Hope and Faith there was no sign. Geoffrey had left Duncraw earlier. The Inspector was eating kippers with obvious relish, and Kenith, toying with mushrooms and bacon, stood up as she came to the table, giving the slight bow with which he favoured all the women. A neighbour at home had told Abigail that adventurers always had beautiful manners but this morning she could not care if Kenith were there to take away the entire library. That inclination of the long, well-shaped head was a tribute to her alone; the slow, dark smile that made her breathless was one he reserved for no one else. Fool, a small voice whispered. He is buried in the country with little diversion and, as he pointed out, there is no unattached girl but for Hope who shies away like a woodland creature, accepting no one.

'How do you manage to keep your subjects still?' she asked, seated with a dish of scrambled eggs topped with a knob of butter and a grinding of black pepper, aware of the dim green of the shrubbery seeming to advance upon the window like the woods of Birnam.

'Certain poses help. An arm laid on a table. The solid, high back of a chair. I have indeed resorted to the use of head clamps – '

'How unpleasant.'

'They would not be necessary in your case. You have the gift of immobility where it is necessary.' His eyes teased her, reminding her of a long, still embrace, only fingers moving very slowly, inducing a voluptuous possession that continued long afterwards.

She sighed, suddenly. It would not last. He would take his ultimate picture, bestow his conclusive, nostalgic kiss. The big, histrionic van would make its final dash down the long drive and all would be as it was – sans parents – sans amis – The sensation of bodily enjoyment faded as a bad portrait degenerated to a dingy brown. A world that had been shown to her, in which colours and textures of infinite richness existed, dwindled to the reality of a hostile room in which Pringles moved like unkempt ants and the dregs of romance were overlaid by the pungent aroma of kippers.

The Inspector wiped at his moustache with a handkerchief that seemed stained with chloride – he had obviously come into contact with Martin's photographic equipment – sighed, though not for the same reason that Abigail had done so – and rose to begin his unpopular task. She did not envy him. He must question the dissenting, look upon the face of disharmony, take upon himself the guise of pariah, knowing that at every move, the household, with infinite stealth, sought to conceal its shabby secrets.

'Remember,' Martin said incongruously. 'If I can help you – '

The Inspector shrugged brusquely. 'I might as well take your pictures.'

Kenith laughed and the load of uncertainty was lifted from Abigail. Charity left as soon as the Inspector had gone, saying she must find something that had fallen behind the furniture in her bed-chamber. They were alone in the shadowy room with Birnam woods threatening the french window in green, misty ranks and the food on their plates hardly touched.

'I should take the study of you. I fear I must have my hands occupied, Miss Abigail Menory, or they will want to do things I must not.'

'There will be no one to stop us from using the Peacock Room today. Charity knows where the key is kept. I heard sounds from it – or imagined I did – and she took me to see it. That was the first night I was here.'

'Indeed!'

'But the room was locked. And empty.'

'The sounds? What were they?'

'Very low voices. It must have been the effect of wind in the chimneys, or sound carried under floorboards. I've thought about it since. That was before I heard the story of the vanished bride – Felicity Croser Scott – otherwise I might have thought myself influenced.'

'I saw her gravestone yesterday. And Miss Hope at her mother's. Ah, there comes the sun! And it's in the right quarter for the Peacock Room. Stay as you are. The yellow will contrast with the darkness of the panelling and your hair must be as it is, loose and shining – '

He made it sound rare and precious. She wanted, quite violently, to feel his hands on it.

'Do you think I could borrow some strong men?' Kenith asked of Hod who was busy at the sideboard. Abigail wondered when he had come back. The room had been empty a short time earlier. Hod had the soldierly quality of moving soundlessly.

'Certainly, Mr Martin. Two or three?'

'Two would be adequate. And the key to the Peacock Room.'

'What do you intend?'

'To photograph the famous bed and the wall carvings. I have license to include what I will. Your men need not stay once the equipment is there. I'll manage better without.'

'Very well.'

'It is to the left-hand side of the van. Anything there is wanted. Ignore the rest.

'There is a turquoise blue love-seat in one of the rooms,' Kenith said after Hod had gone to muster his small detachment. 'It would make a perfect prop. Perhaps for the two Scott girls – '

'You'd never get them in the same quarter.'

'Perhaps Miss Charity and her fiancé?'

'I'm doubtful.'

'I could train the Inspector to take you and me.'

'To what end?'

'A reminder?'

As if she would need any memento of last night. Nothing would ever be the same. She pushed away the remainder of the eggs, the unfinished drink. 'Anyway, you are here to photograph things, not people.'

'I prefer people. Some people –'

'Those thumps and bumps on the stair. That must be your valuable paraphernalia.'

'God's teeth. And I promised –'

'Promised what?'

'Oh, never mind. Come, wood-nymph, sea-sprite, druidical maiden. Grainne of the white birds –'

'I should not have suspected Irish blood in you.'

'Oh, damn all Pringles!'

She scrambled after him, seeing only his long, elegant back, the grey of his coat. Grey. The word was a shaft of warning – a bolt from a reiver's bow.

'You dropped nothing?' he demanded.

'Nothing.' The ape-like faces registered a subdued satisfaction. Martin felt in his pockets for coins which were quickly gathered into hairy paws.

They were alone. The key turned with a grating sound. The splendour of the painted peacock, the myriad shimmering eyes, opened up before them. Hamlet screamed from the terraces below. Or she thought it was Hamlet. There was something queerly human in the sound.

'Sit on the bed,' Kenith said and now his tone was businesslike. 'Lean against the back, as though you were the bird and the spread tail surrounded you. Yes. That seems perfect. Now can you keep the posture for a few minutes?'

'I think so. I wonder where Charity is? Surely she should have found what she dropped? I thought she'd be fascinated by the entire proceeding.'

'Forget Miss Charity. Try to remember how you felt last evening. At about nine o'clock.'

A warm colour infused her cheeks. A small smile upturned her mouth.

She watched him put the black cloth over his head. He was gone and she saw only the gleaming lens, the struts of the tripod, legs and arms grown shadowy, disembodied. She was attacked by unease. 'Kenith?'

'Don't move.' There was a strong smell of chemicals and she wanted to sneeze.

It seemed impossible that a box could capture her likeness so that even as an old woman she would look no different than at this moment. She could understand the awe of primitive peoples at the thought of a stolen image, of their facsimile being owned by a stranger who might sell them to the Devil.

He emerged after a time and it was as though she were reprieved. 'When will I see it?'

'Oh, in a day or two.'

'I must go and fasten up my hair.'

'Must you?'

She nodded. 'I'll find you afterwards. I promise.'

She left him absorbed in the camera and plate and met the Inspector in the passageway. He seemed hardly to notice her and his appearance was quite dishevelled.

Back in her room, she wound up the mass of hair and confined it with pins and a tortoiseshell comb. She was turning from the mirror when she saw the letter propped up on the mantelpiece. She frowned and went to pick it up. Charity's writing, clear and a little schoolgirlish. Or it looked like Charity's –

Abigail tore open the envelope. Her face whitened still further. 'Oh, no,' she whispered. 'Oh, no! no –'

But there was no mistake.

FOUR

She could not think what to do. Scott had left. Not that she would have wanted to break the news that Charity had gone rather than face marrying her cousin, but the necessity of doing so was at least removed until nightfall – until the following day if she were in bed when Sir Humphrey returned.

If she could follow Charity, she might persuade her to return. It would mean going to Cauldshiel, but the Youngs could hardly hang her at the tower. She began to take off the gown and put on her habit. Suzy was at her disposal. Scott had told her she could take the mare whenever she wished. With luck, the stable might be empty of Pringles. She must warn Charity that she knew about the jade statuette and that the Inspector, unless he were an utter fool, could stumble upon her part in the thefts. Charity's disappearance must start a train of thought in her direction, trigger off all manner of unpleasantness.

Abigail pushed the hard hat over her hair with no regard for the effect and went out of the room very quietly. Martin and the Inspector were still in the Peacock Room, talking very quietly. The sound of her footfalls seemed magnified. She was almost at the bottom of the first stretch of staircase when she heard Kenith's voice quite loud and filled with surprise. 'Abigail?'

A door stood open to her left and she went through it, pushing it almost shut as she heard him running down the steps. Looking around her, she saw that she was in a plain, white chamber, the bed virginal, the furnishings simple. On the white-painted dressing-table was an ormolu mirror and a miniature of a girl who could have been Hope and yet was not her. She looked older, more serene. It was Johanne. Brown hair, brown eyes, the antithesis of all the golden Scott portraits. A vase beside it was filled with a mass of clover blooms, buttercups and harebells. A little shrine –

Abigail, by now acutely uncomfortable, wished that she might become suddenly invisible. The sound of Kenith's urgent footsteps having receded, she edged herself out of the room and made her way to the ground floor. The passageways were all cool and mysterious, a maze from which some Cretan bull might appear, barring her way to safety. She opened a thick dark door to find herself at the back of the house, the corner of the stables just visible beyond a thick hedge of holly and laurel. Grit crunched under her boots as she hastened towards the outbuildings.

The stables were quiet and Suzy seemed pleased to be saddled, trotting out into the sunlight, her pretty head in the air. Hod was by the side of the drive, his eyes narrowed suspiciously. He shouted something but Abigail affected not to hear, only waved and smiled disarmingly then urged Suzy to a gallop. The treetops swirled into a green-blue blur, then she was out on to the road and taking the turn to the Hanging Tower.

She seemed to reach it quite quickly as though, like Birnam woods, it had moved in the night. Suzy, a little unwillingly, was prodded through the stream knowing, it seemed, that this was alien territory. Nothing showed at the blind windows of the peel. Abigail pressed on over the damp, tussocky ground, the horse's hooves making sucking noises as they came out of the bogland.

She saw Cauldshiel at last, crouched in a hollow where crows flew, a thin spinney behind it. There seemed no gardens, just the gaunt house and the encroaching moor, the black, ragged wings encircling –

There were two sandy-haired men riding out to meet her but she did not stop.

'What's your business?' one of them shouted and wheeled to ride alongside Suzy.

'I wish to see the Master of Cauldshiel.'

'Well, ye canna. He's in his bed.'

'It was Mr Colin I meant.'

A hand shot out to take her bridle but she slapped it away. 'I'll not be led like a cow to market! And I'll not go away either. If Mr Colin is not in, I'll wait.'

The other rode behind her so that they flanked her like jailers. The porch of the house yawned like an empty mouth.

'Mr Colin? Mr Colin!' the first man called.

He came so quickly that Abigail knew she had already been seen. He stood on the wide, worn step that looked as though swords had been sharpened along its edge. The stout, functional door bore the marks of dints and abrasions. Once, long ago, it had withstood a siege. Hatless and coatless, the sun shone on white, open shirt and artless curls. His eyes were innocent.

'Why, Miss Menory –'

'Tell your watchdogs to let me be.'

Crichton nodded. The sound of hooves abated. They stared at one another. 'Will you not come down?' he asked. 'You look so condemnatory perched up there, and I at a disadvantage. I'm sure Bessie could manage a dish of tea.'

'I have not come to pay a social call.'

'Indeed?' A hardness permeated eyes and voice. He had not looked so yesterday in Hawick. The look of Greek revels and wine softness had gone. The brown fingers that had touched Charity's twisted the stock of a small whip.

'I have come for Charity.'

'You speak nonsense.'

'She left a note for me.'

'Let me see it.'

She frowned. 'I – cannot. I left it in my room in my haste to change.'

'You are not her keeper.'

'No. Her friend. One who feels concern for her. And I think she is mistaken, running off to you. Perhaps I might have agreed with her at first but now I think you play on her feelings for your own ends – '

'The devil, you do!' His eyes blazed angrily. 'It's none of your business.' Then his expression changed as though he enjoyed the sight of her, so stiff and accusing, her red hair crushed under the shiny hat.

'So – you have a small opinion of me. Well, my shoulders are broad. I can bear the blow. But you'll not dictate to me, even if you do feel yourself to be in the right.'

'Charity is here. I know it. Just as I know you followed us yesterday – '

'You saw me? I fancied I did not show myself.' He looked mortified.

'I saw you by the fountain.'

'And kept it to yourself?'

'So you *have* seen her. You'd not have made the last remark if you hadn't. I did not enlighten her.'

His mouth twisted. 'What a clever young **lady** it is. Either go away or come inside.'

She dismounted immediately and held up the skirts of her habit out of the dust around the step. The cuts in the stone looked more brutal than ever. More like hacks than the signs of sharpened steel. Duncraw was a showplace. This was real, had not changed in a hundred years.

Crichton held out his hand and Abigail ignored it.

'You find me so distasteful?'

'I hate what you are doing to Charity.'

'You presume, Miss Menory.'

The shadows of the house enclosed them like widows' weeds. 'Bessie!' Crichton called. A stout woman in black appeared, her sandy hair drawn back into a tight, unbecoming bun. She stared suspiciously at Abigail.

'A dish of tea, Bess. And some of your shortbread.'

'I'm not hungry.'

'Just the tea, then,' he ordered carelessly and shrugged.

They went into a long, dusty room where everything was faded into an almost uniform yellow-brown. The ceiling was part concealed by deep, wide beams and a seat encircled the bay window, cushioned with corded velvet. An open book lay upon it, the back olive-green with a glint of gold. Crichton picked it up and restored it to a crude shelf where other books leaned drunkenly against one another as if for support. Something about the action had a kind of familiarity. Or it might have been the appearance of the book.

Crichton indicated a chair and Abigail, straight-backed, sat down, her lips compressed.

Colin lolled back in another, his hands linked behind his head, smiling infuriatingly.

'Well, Miss Abigail? When do your propose to read the Riot Act? I am not good at suspense. If I have a parcel I must open it immediately – '

'Like you did the parcel Charity gave you yesterday?'

'I'll swear you have eyes in the back of your head.

Charity was careful to pick a table where you'd see nothing.'

'Neither would I, had you not been brought to my notice by other diners who knew you.'

'So that was the way of it. Ah, Bess. Put the tray there, beside Miss Menory. She shall pour.' The woman did as she was bid, her curious stare taking in the cut of Abigail's garments, her green eyes and the strands of bright hair that escaped from under the hat.

Abigail poured the tea. Surely if Charity were here she'd have come in by now? She'd not said it was Cauldshiel she was running to but the implication was there. Crichton picked up the cup – surprisingly fine and delicate compared with everything else she'd so far seen – and said, 'Now listen to me. And do not interrupt.'

She listened.

It had turned cloudy when she returned to Duncraw. The Hanging Tower was shrouded under dark wings of shade and a crow jeered from the bartizan. How odd to be in a place where even the birds were hostile. A few days ago she had seen only the outward beauty of the Border country. Now she was aware of its other face. Duncraw had begun to frighten her with its eddies of hatred and reminders of long-past feuds and fatalities. Felicity Croser and Johanne Scott had become almost more real than Scott's daughters. She thought of Charity with a pity intermingled with envy. Crichton was eminently attractive. Geoffrey had never stood a chance against him. Even if Colin were not wholeheartedly in love with his enemy's daughter, Charity imagined him to be, and her reception of him would be based on the supposition. Her feelings would be as real as though Crichton were all she wanted him to be. She could not blame Charity. Women saw only what they wished to. She herself could be as gullible where Kenith Martin was concerned because he knew how to play upon her need to be desired, because of her essential loneliness. He had only to touch her hair to induce that deadly weakness that could lead, so easily, to a submission she could welcome even as she tried to repudiate it. A man's fingers, the tone of his voice, real or illusive, could reduce any woman to a kind of slavery she afterwards regretted bitterly. How to distinguish the true from the illusive, that was the secret.

The house repelled her as it came into view. The pink stone, the encarmined marble that encircled the terraces, were too pretty for what they half-concealed. The wall of the graveyard drew her. She dismounted, tethered Suzy to a branch and went into the quiet rectangle where the Scotts and Pringles lay in their eternal rest.

A shadow fell across the unkempt mound. She started. It was Peter Rutherford who stood there, quiet and serious in grey coat and twisting his hat between restless fingers.

'There has been quite a search party –'

'Oh!' She stared at him, seeing more in his face than there had previously been. 'I did not think anyone knew –'

He frowned. 'Knew? Knew what, Miss Menory?'

She had been stupid. She thought he meant Charity, when it was her they sought. She'd promised Kenith she'd be with him directly, then Hod had seen her ride away.

'That I had experienced a wish to be alone. It can be difficult to explain.'

'I think I understand. I suppose one could describe me as a solitary.'

Abigail thought she preferred Peter away from other

people. He did look quite kind and there were traces of his mother's good looks if one studied him carefully, though without her hardness.

'Would you find that a disadvantage? Being a doctor?' she asked.

'I don't think so. So long as there was a part of the day I could call my own.'

'My father was like that. I suppose it must be time for luncheon. Should we go back, do you think?' The grey wings of the cloud shadows lay more emphatically on the angled stones and she was reminded of mortality.

'I suppose so.' They walked to the gate. 'I suppose Miss Charity has gone back to the house?'

Suzy stumbled on the track giving Abigail a breathing space. 'Charity? She is visiting a friend I do not know and so I decided to remain behind.' It was true as far as it went. Though she had suspected the girl to be at Cauldshiel, she had not seen her there. Charity might have left a note for someone else.

She left Peter Rutherford by the stables and saw that the mare was safely housed. She wanted to see Kenith and yet she could not bear to let him detect the urgency she felt, so she took her time, wandering slowly to the back door of the house, climbing the stair in a leisurely fashion, disappointed when he did not spring out like a jack-in-the-box to scare her or make her laugh.

She removed the hard hat and the habit and put back the yellow gown. Brushing her hair, she noticed there was something missing from the dressing-table. At first she frowned, unable to place the vanished object. Then she remembered. It was Charity's letter.

There were only men at luncheon. Peter abstracted, the Inspector secretly agitated, judging by the state of his beard and whiskers, and Kenith unsmiling as though he held it against Abigail that she had deserted him without explanation. No one mentioned Hope, and though the letter from Charity had been purloined, no one spoke of her. Perhaps Peter had already passed on Abigail's fictitious reason for the girl's absence.

Martin's coldness depressed Abigail. It had been so pleasant to be on his sunny side and now that he had withdrawn, she felt like an African transported to Lapland. She ate the cold food, her mind tormented by pictures of people in love, of Charity and Crichton by the fountain, white and brown fingers briefly interlaced, Charity's drowning expression under the brim of her bonnet. Eleanor laying her hand on Scott's forearm.

'I saw you and Mr Rutherford come down from the graveyard,' Kenith said.

'Did you?'

'Where did you go?'

Hod lifted his head from his scrutiny of the silver on the sideboard. She could not say she had been to Cauldshiel. That would be tantamount to treachery.

'Oh, here and there. There's much to see. I'm surprised you noticed us. Have you not enough to do with Sir Humphrey's inventory?'

'One must study the light.'

'Of course.' Their glances met and were not friendly. Abigail was attacked by a chill of loss.

'Perhaps we could explore the grounds this afternoon,' Peter said. 'There's a bridge my mother mentioned. A stepping bridge.'

'I shall be glad to accompany you,' Abigail told Peter. 'Perhaps you would care to photograph us, Mr Martin? Of course, the equipment is so heavy it could take all day to position it.'

Martin gave her a look of dislike. 'I'll promise nothing. One expects undertakings to be met.'

'And so they usually are – ' she began.

'Until some other attraction takes precedence.' Martin rose, bowed coldly, and left the room. The Inspector followed quickly.

Abigail went back to her room to fetch her bonnet and found the door of the Peacock Room open and all the vast paraphernalia of the bed exposed. A fire had been lit and the voluminous and surely newish mattress propped before it to begin its airing. Blankets were spread over the chairs. More carving could now be seen against the denuded wall, the lower extremities of the peacock, its feet straddling leaves and acorns, flowers growing up from the skirting board, thrushes and greenfinches pecking and preening. Jeannie and Mrs Davison were beating the dust from the pillows, aided by Meg Pringle. No one had time to notice Abigail.

So Eleanor really meant to sleep in the Peacock Bed. Abigail was conscious of disquiet. She took up her bonnet and went, dispiritedly, to meet Peter. The afternoon was still cloudy though every now and again great shafts of light speared the house and its environs.

They discovered the walled garden filled with massed flowers and the buzzing of insects. A greenhouse of alarming size housed a vine and all manner of seedboxes. Abigail thought she saw Hope's face in the thick, green shadows but when she moved forward there was no sign of the girl.

Leaving the glass-house and the cultivated garden, they followed one of the many paths that led from the main house. Hod was back in the grounds, almost as though he watched them. He had become something of a jailer. Wherever she was, so was Pringle. And yet the thefts could not concern her. They had occurred before her arrival.

The noise of water impinged upon her consciousness. It was a part peaceful, part warning sound, gurgling and choking like some strangled reiver, then giggling as though at some secret joke. Peter said little, his attention fixed on the plants and trees as if he had some interest in botany, his gaze seizing upon a butterfly as it clung to warm stone. He gave the impression of being very far away. It was as though she walked alone. Kenith probably imagined them quite animated and pleased with one another's company.

She saw the bridge quite suddenly, the shape of it like the gables of a Scots cottage. And, as though she had evoked his presence, saw Martin at the other side of the stream, the grey cape flapping in the breeze through the wood.

She forgot Peter Rutherford, his restful quietness. Almost running, she mounted the first step, then another, meeting Kenith at the top, seeing nothing but the dark, crooked smile that surely depicted triumph.

'I came to apologize,' he said.

'There was no need. I did make a promise I did not keep. But it was not because of Mr Rutherford. I only saw him minutes before we came down to Duncraw from the cemetery.'

His fingers reached out to touch hers. Dark fingers like his smile, his long Stuart face, hers white and thin. The memory of Crichton and Charity returned, disturbing her.

'She's gone,' she told Martin without knowing why she must. 'She did not say where.'

'You mean Charity Scott?'

'She – refused to be dragooned into accepting Geoffrey.'

'As you would not be forced into unwelcome matrimony,' he said.

'No.' His gaze hypnotized her like the murmur of the water below them.

'We should wish, now that we are here.'

It's a lovers' bridge, she wanted to say. Only lovers have the right. But that would be arrogance. She closed her eyes and felt the touch of his fingers intensified.

'Have you wished?' he asked.

'Yes.' Her eyes, reopened, looked around for Peter but he was no longer in sight. 'You have not brought your camera.'

'Damn all camera obscuras – all lithographs and daguerrotypes – and blast all Pringles. I want to kiss you but Hod rustles in the bushes. I believe he is torn between watching us or following Rutherford. Did – did Rutherford say anything to you? Anything about his past? Himself or his mother?' The laziness had gone out of his voice.

'Nothing. Only that he is solitary.'

'And Scott?'

'He seems reconciled to accepting his mother's choice.'

'Where did you search for Charity?'

'Cauldshiel.'

'And?'

'I cannot betray confidences.'

'But you did not see the girl?'

She frowned. 'No. I confess I expected to, and cannot quite understand why I did not –'

'But the personable Mr Crichton allayed your fears.'

'I had not realized you had met him.' Abigail felt again that vague disturbance.

'Did I say I had? Ah, you picked up on the adjective. Hearsay, I'm afraid. I asked.'

'I see. You told the truth when you said you were guilty of curiosity.'

'I am guilty of other things. Why are you taking your hand away?'

'This place is too public. Too compromising.'

'Who do you think is taking Sir Humphrey's objets d'art?' he asked unexpectedly.

Abigail flushed.

'So you *do* suspect someone.'

'It is none of our business,' she reminded him sharply. 'That's for the Inspector – and for Scott. In any case, I may not be able to stay to hear the end of the investigation –'

'Why not?'

'Because Charity does not intend to come back. She told me so in a note – ' For some reason she remembered the handwriting that had looked like, yet unlike, Charity's. Disturbance could have made her write more quickly, more carelessly.

'May I see it?'

'Someone took it from my room. But what interest could it have for you?'

'The Inspector has sought my aid. He is intimidated by Pringles and must have one ally.' Kenith stepped over the apex of the little bridge and stood beside her.

'I thought he disapproved of you.'

'Well, he still despises me for the triteness of my vocation. But a man must have a confidant and I am the most convenient. I'm afraid it annoys him that the staff unburden themselves more to me than to him.' Martin chuckled.

'You are altogether too pleased with yourself,' Abigail said severely.

'It is that Puritan streak that draws me. I cannot abide coyness. But you must not go yet. Promise you'll stay till you are asked to leave. Sir Humphrey can hardly throw you out. But take my advice, do not tell him you know anything about his daughter's disappearance.'

'Whoever took the note could tell him.'

'Don't let's cross that bridge until we must. I found the stepping-bridge very agreeable.'

She smiled, then became serious. 'It could be very uncomfortable when everyone returns and Charity's absence is noticed. They will all be beside themselves. Scott, her Aunt Faith. Geoffrey. Oh, there's Hope.'

Martin followed the direction of her gaze. Hope was running up the hillside as though beset by devils, her long brown hair blowing out behind her. She passed between the gateposts that led to the cemetery. A moment later Rutherford came into sight, his head bent as he laboured up the incline and followed her inside, the grey of his coat suddenly obtrusive. Grey. The colour the gipsy had warned her against, Abigail thought. But that might have been the cunning of it, the fact that grey was such a commonplace colour.

'A singular meeting,' Martin murmured. 'I wonder what they will make of one another?'

'Who?'

'Why, Miss Hope and Peter Rutherford. Who else?'

Abigail did not see Hope and Peter again until supper. Aunt Faith had returned with some rolls of material. Apparently Miss Finlay would come out herself later on to take some fittings with Faith's difficult niece. Hope must have something new and be persuaded to attend the weddings.

Abigail's heart sank. There would be at least one missing bride. Faith had asked her rather crossly where Charity was and she had said only that the girl was visiting a friend she could not name.

'Did you not think it odd when it was *she* invited

you?' Faith asked as if this would have been the last thing she, herself, would have thought of.

'Not at all. We are all free agents.' Abigail, looking up, surprised the sly smile that came over Martin's face.

Aunt Faith did not question the Inspector, who, as usual, applied himself to his meal in a fog of abstraction.

Even Kenith Martin seemed a little withdrawn, more of a stranger than a man who had kissed Abigail, and held her hand at the stepping-bridge before submitting her to a cross-examination.

The rumble of the carriage wheels was heard sooner than any of them expected. The uneven grumbling rattled the sashes of the windows.

'I'm sure Humphrey said he'd not be here to supper,' Aunt Faith said agitatedly.

'Then you must not get in such a tizz,' Geoffrey told her, apparently emboldened by the anticipation of his possession of Charity.

They were all eating, rather uneasily, the summer fool Mrs Davison had concocted between her bouts of airing the Peacock Bed, when Scott and Eleanor came in. Immediately, Abigail sensed an aura of disharmony between them. There had been some quarrel during the long day in Edinburgh. The tightness of Mrs Rutherford's pretty lips, the angry colour in the laird's face and his evasive gaze were sufficient to point out this unexpected truth. Why had they been in disagreement? Abigail would have given her soul to know. Then Hod came back with soup dishes on a tray, and all of Eleanor's jealous dislike was plain. She would not countenance her husband's dependence on the Pringles in general and Hod in particular. And, since the laird had already announced his betrothal to the lady, he was in a cleft stick. A gentleman must abide by his declaration if he were honourable and, in this day and age, honour was supremely important.

Impassively, Hod served the soup while Faith apologized miserably for starting without them.

'There's no need to be abject,' Sir Humphrey almost snarled. 'And where's Charity?'

There was a silence, then the Inspector said, 'I'm afraid your daughter has left home. I was going about my duties when I saw a note that said she had decided she could not marry her cousin and must therefore go away. She did not say where she was going but – '

'Colin Crichton!' the laird shouted, looking quite choleric. 'And I forbade that. I told her she must never countenance such an alliance. That the Scotts and Crichtons should marry – it's the rankest deception – a spurious approach from Crichton to turn the head of a silly girl who cannot see she is being used. I should not be surprised – ' He stopped abruptly and relapsed into a brooding silence. The soup grew cool, then cold.

'This note – where did you find it?' Scott asked at last.

'In Miss Menory's room.'

Everyone looked at Abigail. She flushed and prepared herself for condemnation.

'Is this true?' Sir Humphrey asked.

'She did leave me a note. This morning. Out of a sense of loyalty – we were taught this quality at school as you must have been in the army – I could not bring myself to – to say anything until your return. I was bracing myself for the difficult task – '

'I see. Yes, Miss Menory. Loyalty does count. To oneself. To others. I can see what a difficult position you were made to suffer. It's not you I blame. It's Charity – ' Scott continued to glare down at the now-undrinkable soup as though it had done him some injury. 'False child,' he almost whispered.

'And what about me?' Geoffrey asked suddenly, his voice high.

'What about you?' Scott asked cruelly.

'I was to be – Charity's husband.'

'Well, now you will not,' Scott replied, shrugging. 'Hod? Will you bring me a decanter into the study? Proceed without me. Excuse me, Eleanor.' He bowed perfunctorily and went off in the direction of his sanctum where not even Mrs. Rutherford would dare follow, not if she had sense. Hod went after him.

No one paid any more attention to the gooseberry fool, so green and tempting under the splotch of fresh cream, to the cheese and biscuits, or the pyramid of fruit that made up the table's centrepiece. Mrs Rutherford, looking alternately downcast and triumphant, Faith, pale as ashes, and Geoffrey, their futures barren, sat glumly. Hope left the room unchidden, for no one noticed her but Abigail and Martin.

Mrs Davison came into the room and looked in vain for her master.

'Yes?' Mrs Rutherford said waspishly as if already she were mistress. 'What is it?'

'The room is ready. I'd have thought it would take longer but it's done, ma'am. If you'd like to use it tonight we can shift your things now. I've stone bottles in it from head to foot to make sure.'

Eleanor Rutherford smiled her cat smile. Abigail had never seen anyone before with dimples that menaced. It was a stupid fancy but she had never cared for Peter's mother.

'The Peacock Room? Is ready?'

'Yes, ma'am.'

'Then, of course, you must move my belongings.' She watched the housekeeper leave.

'Mother,' Peter said sharply, 'are you sure you are being wise?'

Mrs Rutherford looked all innocence. 'Wise?'

'Apart from the fact that it may not be quite aired – there are those other points. The girl in the locked room –'

'You mean the girl *not* in the locked room.' She laughed metallically.

'And the finding of her body in the river. I wish you would not do it.'

'You speak like some foolish girl.'

Peter flushed, controlling himself with an effort. 'I have never liked the idea –'

'But I have, Peter. I have. And I'll do it, approval or no approval.'

He stared at his mother and Abigail saw his misgivings plainly.

'You make far too much of it,' Eleanor said lightly. 'Do you think I am likely to vanish? I thought you more sensible. It's a legend to add interest to the house and give visitors a thrill – They all do it, the owners of famous houses –'

'I have seen her grave. The inscription on her tomb.'

'You have seen a stone that might have been deliberately inscribed years later. That is what I think happened. There's no one left to prove or disprove.' Eleanor shrugged.

'Very well. I cannot stop you.' Peter rose.

'See you in the morning, my dear,' Eleanor's voice mocked. He did not reply.

Mrs Rutherford got up from the table. Her anger with Scott seemed to have vanished under the stimulus of her clash of wills with Peter and the excitement of occupying the carved chamber. 'Good night to you all.' She left in a heavy silence that no one chose to break.

FIVE

Kenith came to Abigail some time later. She had expected to see Jeannie when she went to answer the tap on her door but it was Martin who stood there.

'What do you want?' She kept her voice low. The knowledge that the Peacock Room was inhabited had a restraining effect.

'I thought you might like to see the picture.'

'Picture?'

'Of yourself. On the famous bed.' He carried something behind his back.

'Oh, that. I thought you said it would take a day or two?'

'I was impatient.' An excitement she recognized took control of his voice. She was afraid he would speak too loudly. Eleanor could be asleep but there was nothing like a quarrel for keeping one awake.

'I always champ at the bit and you'd not frustrate me, would you?'

'Please keep your voice down. Remember the famous bed is now occupied.'

'What? Oh, of course.' His eyes glittered as he whispered his reply. 'Five minutes? I know it is not usually done to invade a woman's room, especially at this hour. But you strike me as sufficiently woman of the world not to act as the besieged jeune fille.'

'Let me see the picture.'

'Not until you let me in.' He smiled maddeningly from his superior height.

She knew she should send him away but she was filled with the same urgency. And the photograph was a magnet she could not resist. 'I must be mad,' she said, opening the door wider, glad it did not creak. She closed it softly once he was in the bed-chamber and leaned against it, watching him move across the floor in the candlelight, his gaze on the painted wallpaper, the green penumbra of the room beyond the circle of illumination, the book she had discarded to answer his knock.

A thrill of alarm shot through her. She could see now what he held. A green bottle with a silver cap. 'I suppose,' she said dryly, 'you have glasses in your pockets?'

'How did you guess?'

The low, amused tones enraged her but she managed to hold the anger in check. 'Please go. And be careful not to be seen. I may not be here for long now that Charity has gone, but while I am, I prefer not to be gossiped about –'

'I could have sworn you'd not use that excuse.'

'I do not make a habit of allowing men the freedom of my bedroom. You came under false pretences.' She shivered slightly.

'Oh, come,' he said very softly and sat on the edge of the bed to watch her mockingly. 'You didn't care about the picture. You wanted me to be here as much as I did. Isn't that true?' The movement caused her book to fall to the carpet where it lay, the pages turning idly.

She wanted to repudiate the suggestion but the lie stuck in her throat.

'That's all the answer I need,' he said after a minute and let the bottle fall on to the counterpane. He came to her swiftly and took her in his arms. 'It was a clumsy attempt at best,' he muttered against her hair.

'Attempt?' Her voice shook for all her efforts at composure. She responded to the feel of his body against hers, the sensation of being encircled by something extraordinarily alive. His arms and his hands seemed a separate part of him, holding her, stroking her in a way so pleasurable she'd never be able to tell him to stop.

'At seduction.'

Her head jerked upwards. The dark, smiling eyes had the grace to look ashamed. 'I knew as soon as I saw your face turn pale that I couldn't do it. It's all or nothing with you, Abigail, isn't it? I must confess, I'm still tempted. You couldn't cry out, could you, not with Eleanor Rutherford next door. But,' as he felt her prepare to free herself, 'as I said, I won't force you to act against your wishes. Though –' He was experienced enough to read her expression correctly.

'Please, stop.' Her voice was ragged, too harsh. He knew her feelings exactly. Her pride was dented by the realization that she was not as worldly wise as she had imagined. She was usually mistress of the situation. Ironic to think that for years she had been providing a strong arm for Charity and now the girl had managed things incomparably better. Charity had brought a sophisticate like Colin to the brink of marriage. Where was she now and what was she doing?

Abigail froze. Someone was walking along the hall. Whoever it was moved quietly but purposefully. She might have missed the sound altogether if she had not been pressed right against the door, her cheek laid on the cold smoothness of the panel.

Kenith opened his mouth to say something and Abigail laid her finger across her lips. His brows lifted. The footfalls hesitated and she thought for one blood-freezing moment that they were stopping at her room, but they went on, more slowly, less determinedly. She could not hear them now. There was a tapping noise that was repeated after an interval, then a faint sound of movement, of ensuing voices.

'You must go,' she whispered urgently. 'Someone is with Mrs Rutherford. Her son probably.'

'Or Scott.'

'They quarrelled. Have you forgotten?'

'No. But quarrels can be made up. Reconciliations can be very pleasant.'

She would not look at him. She sighed. 'I wish you had not come.'

'You don't. You were made to feel passion. And you did.' His whisper was unbearably agreeable. She could not deny it. 'You won't change your mind?'

She shook her head. 'I'll see if the passage is clear.' Opening the door cautiously, she peered out. The sound of voices rose angrily. Kenith Martin pressed close beside her, listening.

'Having you criticize Hod was bad enough. We are lifelong comrades, friends. But to suggest that I must send Hope to some kind of a Bedlam! I'll not countenance it,' Sir Humphrey expostulated. 'I'll neither send the Pringles packing, nor despatch my daughter to a lunatic asylum because she clings to the memory of her mother. I have been mistaken in you, Eleanor –'

'But I am to be your wife. You announced the fact before several witnesses. Remember?'

There was a silence.

'I shall find a way out of the quandary,' Scott said eventually, his voice heavy.

'Without losing the famous honour? Ah, I thought that would find a weak spot,' Mrs Rutherford taunted.

'You did not love me at all. It's just Duncraw and the *famille-rose*,' Scott insisted painfully.

'No. It's something much stronger. I'll tell you later. But we must not quarrel so noisily, my dear. That nice girl with the scarlet hair will be tossing and turning in her bed. She could hardly sleep through the shouting. I'm glad I found that wedding-dress today. And I know that I am right about the undesirability of that gamekeeper-cum-butler and all his encumbrances. And that Hope is – unbalanced and must be confined –'

'Eleanor!' All of his rage and detestation was in the cry.

'Now, please go and let me sleep,' Eleanor said with annoying calm. 'We can make further plans when you are less – hostile. You'll come round to my way of thinking.'

'Don't you understand?' Sir Humphrey's voice was bleak. Dangerous. 'You have gone too far.'

'When you have thought it over –'

'There's nothing to think over.'

'You are mistaken, my love.'

There was a sudden crash, the stamp of feet. Just in time, Kenith had swept Abigail inside the room and closed the door. They were fused together for an interminable space while Scott strode noisily down the passageway, then there was a clatter on the stairs, the faint bang of a door. Abigail fancied Mrs Rutherford had laughed. She could not be quite sure but the soft, eerie suggestion of a sound made the hair prickle on her neck. She was trembling now and Kenith was kissing her lips and her throat. She tightened her arms around his neck and his head burrowed against her breast. He would feel her heart thumping shamelessly.

'How – unpleasant,' she said unsteadily.

'Do you mean what I am doing or what we have just heard?'

'What we heard.'

'I'm glad it was not the other way round.'

'It was – awful.'

'Try not to think of it.'

'He must have come to make up the earlier quarrel, then this notion of Hope being – restrained made matters a thousand times worse. It was a very public quarrel. How stupid of her to antagonize him now. Before the wedding – ' Her voice trailed away.

'Quite disgraceful,' Kenith murmured. 'But people cannot always plan their quarrels for the most appropriate time. Life is not like that.'

'Not like seductions? They must be planned in every detail, well beforehand.'

His laughing face made her alive to a new danger. If he did not go soon he was never going at all. And Mrs Rutherford was very much awake. 'You must go. Please – '

'Very well, Miss Menory.'

'The champagne – '

'I will leave it. Hopefully.'

'You might as well take it.'

'No. Hide it in a drawer. The Inspector will find it and take you for a secret drinker.'

'I am not pleased with him. To take *my* letter!'

'He has his job to do. And it was perhaps the easiest way to break the news to Charity's father. That was why you ran off this morning, wasn't it? To look for her?'

'Yes.'

'Good night, then.' He tightened his arm around her waist, then was gone. She went to the doorway after a minute or two had elapsed, thinking she still heard him, and looked down the quiet passage. It was very dark but not too dark to see the outline of a slight figure at the top of the servants' stairs. The faint glow from the Green Room played on the young, sullen face of Hope Scott and the cup she held in one steady hand.

Abigail woke unwillingly, one part of her repressing depression, the other remembering the encounter with Martin, ashamed of the tide of feeling the thought of him aroused. He's an adventurer, she told herself sharply and made herself get up to face the chill of the morning. It had been one of the coldest nights she could remember at this time of year. She hated cold weather as a cat detests wind and rain.

Even in the mirror she looked bleak and a trifle pinched and the severity of the hairstyle she had chosen, in reaction to her feeling for Martin, made her appear older. Quite old, she thought with misgiving. He'd see her as she really was. But wasn't that the point of the exercise? To find out if he still found her desirable stripped of all women's frills? He already knew she had no money worth mentioning. She moved her head impatiently and saw the little curls that had escaped from all her endeavours to subdue them. They twisted upon her neck like small, red snakes, mocking her.

She emerged into the chill of the passage, intent upon procuring a fire in her room. As soon as breakfast was over she'd return to it until she decided what she was going to do. With Charity gone, no one would expect her to stay indefinitely.

She turned, automatically, to pinpoint the place where Hope had stood last night. Light lay on the carpet as though the door of the Peacock Room stood open. Abigail was drawn towards the place irresistibly. The door was, indeed, wide open. Mrs Rutherford must have risen early. She looked into the room and saw everything stirring as though the window too was ajar, the drapes, the long soft grasses in the turquoise vase, the peacock feathers, the stockings that lay over the arm of the bedside chair. Cold air struck her unpleasantly.

Abigail was shocked into a standstill by the sight of a face on the pillow in the morning shadows of the bed itself. Eleanor still lay there under the rich coverings, her bosom bare, one arm hanging white and unmoving over the edge, the fingertips pointing floorwards. The girl stood watching, some sixth sense making her heart thump unevenly. Eleanor was too inert. There seemed no rise and fall of breathing and in spite of the unquiet and obvious discomfort of the room that was exposed to the elements, the curtains swishing angrily as the icy wind tore at them, the woman did not wake.

Thoroughly uneasy, Abigail went inside the chamber and ran to close the window. Instantly, everything became as lifeless as the occupant of the great carved bed. The girl went to Eleanor, feeling for a pulse, alarmed by the coldness of the woman's body, the lack of heartbeat when she explored the pallid bosom. The face was mask-like. Abigail shook her. 'Mrs Rutherford. Mrs Rutherford!' There was no response.

Once certain that the woman was dead, she stood as if paralysed, then forced herself eventually to the decision that she must raise the alarm. She was startled to hear a man's footsteps coming towards the room. Turning her head, her stricken gaze encountered the surprised eyes of Peter Rutherford. Instinctively, in order to cushion the shock, she moved in front of the body.

'What is it?' Peter asked, frowning. 'Why are you here?'

Abigail tried to say something but her mind still would not co-operate.

'Get away!' Peter said roughly and, crossing the carpet, pushed her aside. In a very different tone he said, 'Mother! Mother? What have you done, Miss Menory?'

'No-nothing. I saw the door open as I started to go to breakfast. I looked in – and saw that the window was open. And then I saw – her.'

'Then why try to hide her body?' He straightened up, his face twitching oddly.

'She really *is* dead?'

'She is.' He looked away, a muscle in his cheek flickering. 'Why did you?'

'To save you the shock. But it seems I have not. And why should I want to harm her?' Abigail asked, distressed that he should even think so. 'Why not Sir Humphrey – or Hope?'

Peter stared at her fully then, his eyes narrowed. Too late she realized her mistake. If she had not been so shaken she would never have said anything so damaging. It was obvious now that Peter knew nothing of the quarrel last night. He had probably been asleep. And no one had seen Hope but herself. She began to feel sick.

'Answer me,' he demanded sharply. 'What did you mean?'

'I – I cannot even remember what I said. It has been a dreadful experience. To know that while I slept – she died – '

'Yes,' he replied more gently. 'But you have said it now and I will have to tell the Inspector your exact words. He will ask for an explanation. Now will you leave me? I should like to be alone with her. Just for a little.'

'Of course,' she said mechanically and retreated from the Peacock Room, hearing the door close behind her. She went into her own bed-chamber, numb and chastened, without motive, and stood by the window watching the leaves swirl by on the skirts of the wind and the treetops swaying and sighing with a noise of shingle on a pebbly shore. Eleanor dead. Yesterday she had been healthy and vigorous. Today –

Abigail pushed her way out of the room and blundered towards the staircase. It seemed to take her an age to negotiate the bends and the steps seemed to go on for ever. She must tell Scott. She arrived at the hall distressed and panting. The door of the study was ajar and Abigail thrust at it, hardly knowing what she was doing. She had expected Sir Humphrey to be there and it was disconcerting to find the room empty. It appeared that the laird had left the study in the middle of some task, for a wall cupboard, sandwiched between bookcases, had been left open. Inside it she glimpsed an assortment of objects that, even as she looked at them, assumed an odd familiarity. A book with an olive-green binding that looked exactly like the one she saw at Cauldshiel, replaced on a sagging shelf by Colin Crichton. A miniature of a fair young woman in a large feathered hat, blue-eyed and smiling. Something that could have held tobacco or sweetmeats. Or tea! A very beautiful little snuff-box. A paper-weight. Crystal with even the grey daylight picking out rainbow flashes. Everything that Inspector Moray had on his list of missing articles. Except the statuette, and she knew where that was and who had taken it there. Crichton had spoken the truth. He had told Abigail that the only article Charity had removed from Duncraw was the jade figure which had been left to her by an uncle who travelled in the East. She had not reminded her father of her ownership for the obvious reason that she wished not to draw unfavourable attention towards herself on the eve of flight. Scott had noticed the statue was not in its usual position and had told the Inspector.

But why have a list of stolen property at all? Nothing was gone but Charity's own possession, given to Crichton to sell in order to pay off the more pressing of his debts. Her dowry —

Abigail had almost forgotten Eleanor when the sound of a step made her whirl round. Sir Humphrey stared at her, then at the opened cupboard. A slow flush mounted in his drawn face. 'What the devil!'

'I'm sorry. I came to look for you. I was not prying.'

'No?' The word was insulting.

Abigail turned as red as Scott, then paled again, remembering the corpse upstairs. 'I came to tell you that Mrs Rutherford —'

'Yes?' Scott interrupted. 'What about Mrs Rutherford?' The high colour intensified.

'She's — she's dead.' There seemed no other way to tell him.

Sir Humphrey rocked on unsteady legs. His face had become quite grey. Abigail ran to him and pushed him into a buttoned leather chair that squeaked under his weight. He made a muffled, choking sound that frightened her. 'Hod!' she called out. 'Hod!'

Hod came as if by magic. 'Can you find the brandy?' she asked quickly. 'Sir Humphrey's had a great shock.'

Hod's eyes flicked over the cupboard which contained the objets d'art. His lips pursed. One hairy hand pushed it shut. He moved softly but swiftly to the corner of the room and opened another cabinet, taking out a bottle and glass, then poured a generous drink and took it to Scott. 'Drink that,' he ordered with the Pringle equivalent of kindness. Abigail was unexpectedly touched by the rough emotion. Scott, persuaded into taking several sips, began to look better. Hod stood back.

'Please give me some, too,' Abigail asked. Hod obeyed her without argument.

'What is wrong?' he ventured.

'I'm afraid that Mrs Rutherford died in the night.'

Hod's fingers almost lost their grip on the bottle. He turned away quickly but not before Abigail had seen his expression. She was suddenly cold. It was not the reflex one expected when told of a bereavement. Quite unmistakably, Hod had smiled.

When he turned back again his features were composed in a conventional distress. She took a long gulp and shuddered at the impact. Her eyes watered and tears pricked at her eyes, but she felt better able to cope.

'I take it it was you, miss, who found the body?'

'Yes.'

'I said it was a mistake,' Hod remarked quietly.

'Mistake?' Abigail watched Sir Humphrey's pallor change to a more normal hue.

'To insist on sleeping in that room. It's an unlucky place.'

Abigail had forgotten the legend under the weight of stress and disbelief. 'I'd not thought of the old story. Peter tried to dissuade her last night.'

'Should have listened then, shouldn't she?'

'That's enough, Hod,' Scott said sharply, now apparently in complete command of himself. He pulled himself out of the chair, supporting himself for a moment by gripping the mantelpiece. A spark from the fire sounded like a pistol-shot. Abigail was the only one of the three who started.

'I must go to her.'

'Peter said he wished to be alone with her for a little.'

'Peter? What's he got to do with it?'

'He came up to speak to Mrs Rutherford and found me there beside the bed. The door and window were wide open and the wind was blowing in –'

'Not like that other one, then,' Hod said. 'That Jacobite lass – all locked in – '

'Hod. Will you not bring up that old business? Someone must find the Inspector. Oh, and Mr Martin.'

'I'll do that.'

'Send them up to the Peacock Room.'

'Very well.' Hod never said sir, or Sir Humphrey, when replying to his master. But between comrades, as Scott had described their relationship, titles must have no real meaning. They were brothers at arms, always would be now that Eleanor was dead. Abigail, disturbed by the thought, watched Hod go out of the study, a spring in his step.

'Do you wish to come up with me?' Scott asked. 'Though I should imagine it's the last thing you want. Stay here. Have some more brandy.'

'No. I will come. It would be as well to have another woman there in case Hope should hear, or Faith. I'm over the fright, thanks to Hod and the Courvoisier.'

'That's a good girl. I wish Charity had been more like you. She was always so spineless. She'd have been a coward if she'd been a boy. Run at the first shot.' Contempt infused his tones and once again the angry colour rose up in his face.

'She might have surprised you.' Abigail sprang to her friend's defence. 'She'd never have run away if she'd been the milksop you make her out to be.'

Scott gave a noncommittal grunt and made for the stairs.

'I saw those things in the cupboard,' Abigail said quietly, hard on his heels.

He stopped so suddenly that she almost fell backwards. She clutched at his arm. The hard blue eyes bored into hers. 'You'll forget what you saw,' he told her in a soft voice that cloaked anger. 'If you had knocked and waited – '

'Would you? If you were a woman who had just found death in the next room?'

Some of the choler went out of the intimidating stare. 'I don't ask because of any reflection upon myself. There is a very particular reason why no one must know the valuables are found – '

'If they were ever lost,' Abigail could not resist saying. Blame the brandy, the episode with Martin last night, her horrific discovery of half an hour ago.

'Miss Menory. Please!'

She was, unexpectedly, sorry for him. For Scott, the unpleasantness was just beginning. The Inspector would ask what she had meant by that incautious remark to Peter. She would have to answer. Kenith Martin knew what she did and boasted he was the Inspector's confidant. If only she had not mentioned Hope with her bewildered and sulky look and the cup held so rigidly – the cup! 'I'll say nothing,' she said abruptly.

Scott was surprised by her swift capitulation. He nodded, then continued to plod up the stairs. She had thought him completely recovered but his step was that of an old, tired man. They emerged on to the top landing and her heart leapt. She was not sure she could, after all, go inside that room.

She lagged behind, watching the laird's progress, his hand on the knob. He looked back, the sweat beading his forehead, then turned the knob and passed inside the chamber. There was a long silence.

'Are you all right?' she called. The silence persisted so she hurried, staring in at Sir Humphrey's still figure.

The bed was empty.

'Is this some kind of joke?' Scott asked at last, his voice heavy.

'Would I do anything so pointless?'

'I'd hardly think so, but this has been such a madhouse of late. I thought you said young Rutherford was here?'

She stared, dry-lipped, at the empty bed. Everything else was the same, down to that pathetic pair of stockings over the chairarm. 'He was. Do you think he has ordered her — removal?'

'Why? In any case, nothing should have been disturbed. You'd think a doctor would know! And removed where, in God's name? Do you think you were mistaken? That she was simply unconscious and that Rutherford succeeded in reviving her?'

'She was icy cold —'

'You said the window was wide open. There's a wind to freeze Eskimos. And she came to this room too precipitately.'

'I could detect no pulse.'

'You must have been wrong.' Scott went to the bed and tore the covers back as far as they would go. His eyes were tormented. He certainly presented a convincing picture of grief.

'But Peter said she was dead. He must be able to tell.'

'He's a young inexperienced man. Can't know everything.' He began to pace the floor.

'Sir Humphrey. I'd swear —'

'Then where is she?'

The thought came to Abigail that this was too like the disappearance of Felicity Croser Scott, apart from the fact that the room had not, on this occasion, been locked. And where was Peter? As if on cue, the doorway darkened and Rutherford appeared, angrily demanding the reason for the taking away of his mother's corpse. Sir Humphrey looked stupefied.

'We thought — you —'

'Why should I do anything so foolish? I have been gone only a matter of minutes. I was overcome. And I did not want my mother exposed to public gaze so I went to fetch a nightgown from the trunk that was left, inadvertently, downstairs during the flitting from the floor below.' Indeed, the garment hung, shroud-like, over one arm.

'Then Eleanor must be still alive. She's gone to seek aid –'

'My mother is dead. Ask Miss Menory,' Peter said coldly.

'I'm afraid there's no doubt.'

'Then where in the devil is she?' Scott asked again. He looked ill himself, Abigail thought. On top of the blow of losing Eleanor was the mystery of her disappearance. But had it been such a blow? Remembering the violence of last night's quarrel, she was unsure. Scott must be relieved, yet he pretended sorrow. Not like Hod who had grinned at the news. His reaction seemed most honest. No Pringle had cause to mourn Eleanor's passing. She had made no secret of her intentions.

'That's what I want to know,' Peter said grimly, throwing the nightdress over the bed. 'Bodies do not simply vanish into air.'

'It's true that when we got upstairs there was no sign of her. Sir Humphrey and I were together all the time – well, most of the time once I reached the study.' There had been the interval while she made her discovery of the contents of the wall-cupboard. Was Scott protecting someone? Hope seemed the only person for whom he'd dissemble. Or Hod. She could not remember how long she had been alone.

'I am at a loss to explain,' Scott said, shaking his magnificent head like an injured bull. 'In fact, I cannot explain –'

'I informed the Inspector. If I am not mistaken that is his step on the stair,' Peter broke in impatiently. He no longer sounded like a shy young doctor. He appeared, suddenly, to be much older than his years, mouth twisted with bitterness.

The Inspector arrived, as usual flustered. For a man who had traced the murderer of an unknown man and the killer of Mary Emsley, he gave no impression of organization or subtlety, but the sight of his mussed hair and untidy beard was undoubtedly comforting. 'Are *you* all right, sir?' he asked Scott.

'Yes – But this other – ' Scott indicated the empty bed. 'This vanishing trick – '

'Vanishing trick?'

The story of the finding and losing of Mrs Rutherford's body was interrupted at an early stage by the unobtrusive entry of Kenith Martin. Abigail seemed the only person to notice he was there, Scott and Peter intent only on one another and the Inspector's questions. How long had Miss Menory been downstairs? How long before Sir Humphrey joined her in the study? When had Hod come on the scene? Why had Abigail come to the Peacock Room in the first place? Who had been last to see Mrs Rutherford? No one having volunteered an answer to this, Peter said, 'Miss Menory may be able to tell us.'

Abigail's eyes met those of Martin. His, she discovered, were hard and bright, no help to her at all, and his face was cold and absorbed above the collar of a grey coat she had not previously seen. How different he had been, only hours ago –

'Well, Miss Menory?' the Inspector asked inexorably.

'I – would rather not say.'

Inspector Moray gestured grandiloquently, a flourish he had copied from the photographer, she realized, and wanted to laugh. She had to bite her lip to combat the inclination to hysteria. 'You *must*,' he insisted sternly. 'It is a serious matter.'

'When I taxed Miss Menory about her attempt to hide my mother's body she said it was to save me the shock. Then she asked me why she should want to harm my mother. Why not Sir Humphrey, or Hope,' Peter said clearly.

'Did you say that?' Moray asked and ruffled his sandy hair afresh.

She hesitated. 'Yes.'

'Why?'

'Because I heard Sir Humphrey quarrelling with Mrs Rutherford. It was impossible not to hear. I'm sorry Mr Rutherford forced me into telling you. I was shocked at the time and not responsible for my words. I really am sorry – ' She watched Scott apprehensively.

'And Hope?' Peter reminded her, his face drawn for all its vengefulness. It seemed he regretted the necessity of mentioning the girl.

'I looked out into the hall after Sir Humphrey went away. Hope was standing at the top of the servants' stair. I dare say she had heard the quarrel too and was frightened.' She really could not mention the cup. Let the girl tell them herself. She could not get her tongue around it. Eleanor had looked so still, so unmarked, like someone who had taken some strong potion and slept her life away. There had been no sign of a struggle. But perhaps her heart had been weak and she upset by the recent scene –

'Did you hear any sound from Mrs Rutherford after Sir Humphrey left?'

Abigail's skin crept. 'Yes. I thought she laughed.'

'You only thought she laughed?'

'I could not swear to it in a court of law – '

'You may have to,' the Inspector said righteously

then caught Martin's considering gaze upon him. He flushed.

'All very interesting,' Peter sneered, 'but this does nothing to find out what has happened.'

'The house must be searched, obviously,' the Inspector announced, avoiding Martin's eye.

'May I go back to my own room?' Abigail asked. 'In fact, I have to go. I do not feel myself.' She was ashamed to find her body trembling and her head unpleasantly light. She would never forgive herself if she committed the unpardonable folly of fainting. It was the coldness, the lack of breakfast, the horror of the past hour. And Martin's abandonment of her. That had upset her most of all. He had seemed unaware of her feelings apart from that one impersonal glance.

'Of course,' the Inspector said. 'We will leave you undisturbed. I realize this has been an ordeal for you – '

'As it has been for us all,' Peter interrupted. If they did not uncover the truth it would not be his fault. She noticed incongruously that he was sweating.

'I think we need not keep Miss Menory any longer,' Kenith Martin said surprisingly and put out a graceful hand to support her. 'You have nothing more to add to your testimony?'

'N-no.' Her teeth were chattering and she had to clench them hard to stop the betraying sound.

'I'll have Jeannie sent up with some tea,' Scott told her ungraciously.

'Thank you. I should like that.'

'And I also think I should like you to make arrangements to go home since Charity is no longer here.'

'Oh, but that isn't possible,' Martin interposed gently. 'Is it, Inspector?'

'What? Oh, er, no. So long as there is an enquiry

and Miss Menory *is* a vital witness, she must remain here. It was not her fault she heard raised voices, was it? You did, I presume, have words with Mrs Rutherford?'

'We did have a disagreement. Yes,' Scott agreed unwillingly. 'It – it would have resolved itself.'

'Then what has Miss Menory done that is so reprehensible?'

'She has tried to implicate my daughter –'

'If I remember rightly, she placed a very innocent interpretation on Miss Hope's presence. Remember she had been practically accused of harming Mrs Rutherford by Mr Peter and it was in the heat of the moment that she disclosed that others had been on the scene.'

'I suppose so,' Scott replied grudgingly. 'But it seemed a poor return for hospitality.'

'Sir Humphrey, the laws of hospitality are null and void where unexpected death and inexplicable disappearance are concerned. There can be no connection. It is fact and the truth that count and must be divulged under the severest penalties for concealment.'

'Yes, I see,' Sir Humphrey said more quietly. 'Forget what I said, Miss Menory. Jeannie will be told to come up to see you.'

'You'd better include a hot brick,' Kenith said, touching Abigail's hand. 'The girl has a chill. Shall I come with you?' This to Abigail.

'No, thank you. I'd rather manage by myself.' She moved away blindly, glad to be rid of portentous glances and questioning. The voices receded and the green gloom of her own room enclosed her in a dispassionate tranquillity. She stumbled to the armchair and sank into it, her nails pressed into her palm. Their sharp bite represented reality. Her senses swam, returned into frigid focus. The morning was filled with faint footfalls, running steps.

Jeannie came after an age had passed, a laden tray in her hands. She plonked it down on the low table and taking the flannel-wrapped brick from under her arm she thrust it into the bed. 'Get some of that tea inside you, Miss Abigail. Has that woman really disappeared?' She knelt to put a light to the fire.

'You should say Mrs Rutherford. After all she is dead.'

'It's that room. Right from the moment Mrs Davison said it was to be put ready, a cold grue came over me. Fussed about the bed like an old hen she did, making us change the mattress, putting things under the pillow and between the sheets –'

'Things?'

'Herbs and lavender. Hypocrisy really, 'cos she didn't like her any more than the rest of us. Took her a hot drink too.' The sticks were crackling cheerfully and the coal was alight.

Abigail sat up sharply. 'When was that?'

'Oh – it must have been bed-time. Mrs Rutherford liked it just before she blew out her candle. She's been took, like that girl was. No one should ever go in that bed again. After all, she was a bride even if she was a bit long in the tooth. That room has something against brides.'

'I don't feel like the rest,' Abigail said, wanting nothing more than to be left alone. 'Just take the tray, please, Jeannie. The Inspector says I can be undisturbed so I'll try to go back to sleep. Thank you for lighting the fire.'

'And the bed's nice and warm.' Jeannie hesitated, the tray balanced expertly. 'It gives you the creeps, doesn't it, not knowing – where it is.'

'Where what is?'

'The body.'

Abigail shivered involuntarily. 'Yes, it does. Thank you, Jeannie.' Her tone was firm enough to constitute a dismissal, yet after the girl had gone she was conscious of a sense of loneliness. She took off her gown and got between the sheets in stays and petticoats. The brick was deliciously cosy against the soles of her feet. Gradually she became comforted and drowsy. She had almost forgotten why she was here like a skulking invalid. Eleanor's white face and motionless fingers had receded into a beckoning limbo where she was swallowed up completely.

SIX

The door of the Peacock Room was closed. Abigail went to it and turned the handle, but it was now locked and with it its gruesome secret. She stood, considering. Why had she not seen Charity at Cauldshiel? Was it because she had never left Duncraw? Had she decided there was too much risk in a second marriage for her father? Mrs Rutherford was in her forties but she had looked strong and healthy and it was not impossible that she might have produced a son. And, although Sir Humphrey's first impulse was to disinherit his daughter, he might have had second thoughts. Or had Crichton had a finger in the pie? If there had once been a passage in use between Duncraw and Cauldshiel, might it not have been a temptation to dispose of the woman who had insisted on using the room where a Crichton bride had once, most certainly, been murdered then tossed into the river? But the first thing warring families would have ordered would be the destruction or barring of means of access. That seemed elementary.

It could, of course, have been reopened.

She heard the sound of hooves and went to the window at the end of the hall. From her point of vantage she saw several Pringles, uncouth and shaggy, each with a fowling-piece and mounted on equally rough ponies. With a curious thrill, she realized that this was how their ancestors must have looked two hundred years ago, the morning mist dimming their crude shapes into anonymity, their movements purposeful. But, instead of remaining in a long file as they would have in the reiving days, the crouched figures separated and trotted, very slowly, in different directions. They'd be searching the grounds for Eleanor Rutherford.

Disturbed, she began to descend the stairs, then started back as she saw two shadows on the wall below. Faith's voice floated upwards, soft and controlled. 'Well, that's half our worries out of the way.'

'Mother – '

'Oh, don't mother me. That's always been your attitude, hasn't it, and look where it's got you. If you'd asserted yourself with Charity – '

'Mind your own business!' Geoffrey said with a repressed venom. 'I *will* get her back even if I've to use force to do it.'

'Geoff!' Faith could not have sounded more surprised if he'd turned into a snake.

'Can you never leave *anything* be? I loved Charity.'

'No one asked you to love the girl. Just to marry her and you couldn't even manage that.'

The voices had risen incautiously. Made prudent by the realization, Faith said, almost in a whisper, 'We won't have to worry about her again. Mrs Interfering Rutherford.'

'Do you think they'll find her?'

'I should think so. But if they do, what difference could it make now? She's dead. We'd best not stand here too long, talking. What you should be doing is trying to get hold of Charity before she commits herself.'

Might as well try to stop the tide, Abigail reflected. If Charity felt about Crichton as she did about Martin, she'd have committed herself long ago. And, judging by her expression in Hawick, the girl was besotted.

She went into the withdrawing-room, attracted by the cheerful pattern of reflections from the firelight that danced upon the walls. She was discomfited to find the room was not, as she had first thought, empty. Hope was crouched in a chair, close by the back window, her eyes on the mounted Pringles who still rode close by the house. Starting visibly at Abigail's entry, she jerked herself upright.

'I'm sorry. Did I startle you?'

Hope shook her head and made as if to rise.

'Oh, don't go,' Abigail said reassuringly. 'I only came to warm my hands. To tell the truth, I feel like a fish out of water. Not really belonging, but unable to make a dignified exit.'

The girl still said nothing.

'I hope I did not frighten you last night? I imagined I heard some sound –'

'No. I wasn't afraid.'

'It was nothing, you know. Everyone quarrels at some time or other –'

'Mother never quarrelled with him! Or with anyone –'

'Mothers are usually careful not to allow their children to become aware of friction in case it erodes their security. But that's a very different thing from never being at loggerheads. It just isn't natural for anyone with spirit not to have differing views from their partner. I think I'd find it very dull being dutiful and submissive *all* the time. Quarrels can clear the air.'

'Not that sort of quarrel. She must have known that he – that I –'

'It certainly wasn't very clever of her,' Abigail said carefully, 'but I think she may have meant it for the best. Isn't it time you thought more about the present than the past? I admire loyalty but there comes a time when it becomes obsession. It's a pity you weren't sent to school like Charity.'

The brown eyes grew wider and darker. The soft lips parted.

'You recognized how pleasant it was when your parents were – a couple very wrapped up in one another? You're a pretty girl. It's time you looked around you for a young man. I think Peter likes you –'

'He's that woman's son!'

'He's an individual. There comes a time when the umbilical cord becomes a chain and a fetter. I think you know this and that you are rebelling against that knowledge, making histrionic demonstrations against it. Isn't that true?'

Hope hunched her shoulders as against an unwelcome chill. 'I – don't know.'

'But I do. It's time to start forgetting. Renewing everyday life instead of blowing on old memories to resurrect the flame that's better dead. It's not too late.' Abigail rose from the hearthrug and rubbed her hands. 'You'll think I'm an interfering woman but I do mean it for the best. Charity was very sensible now I've had time to think it over. She's living for someone else and not inside herself. Think about it.' She started for the door. 'Why not tell your father he is being unfair to Charity for a start? He might listen to you. And it is true, however strongly you feel about him. Wouldn't it be better if you were a real family? Not just pieces of a jigsaw puzzle that will never fit because there's something vital missing? I'll see you later, Hope.'

Peter Rutherford was outside as she left and she wondered how long he had been there. Something in his expression told her she'd said the right things, something else stopped her from speaking to him. She turned in time to see him going into the room where she had left Hope. Whatever he felt for Sir Humphrey's fey child, he'd never try seduction. She felt it in her bones and warmed to him. Apart from this morning, he'd been – nice. An inadequate word. His pallor touched her.

Mrs Davison was emerging from the study. Abigail looked at her closely. Tall and well-made, the woman was an imposing figure in her black gown and white cap, the bunch of keys jangling from the belt at her waist. Did she have a copy of the key to the Peacock Room? It did not seem unlikely. Abigail remembered what Jeannie had said about the recent preparations to the Peacock Bed. Herbs and lavender. What if there had been something else? What about the bed-time drink? Pringles stuck together. There could have been another secret conclave like the one that had resulted in Mrs Davison's post as housekeeper. Long straws and short. But no one knew how Mrs Rutherford had met her end. It might have been due to natural causes, but why the open window and door? No one in their right senses would have left them open on such a night. There had been a case she had read in which the room had been kept very hot in order to disguise a time of death. What if this had been an attempt to do the same, only in reverse? Abigail was sure the Inspector must already have thought of this. What an odd little man he was, but judging by his record in detection, a force in his own field.

She had a sudden longing for fresh air, to reassure herself about Charity. Mrs Davison had taken herself off kitchenwards. Abigail opened a side door and found that the weather was warmer so she ran upstairs for her cloak and bonnet and went out into the garden. It might not be possible to use Suzy today but no one could object to her taking a stroll. Walking through the path between the laurels she heard the distant sound of hooves, slow and careful.

The lawns opened out, bordered by bushes bearing yellow flowers. The house stood in the lee of the long, gradual hill, quiet and passive, the pink shadowed with blue, the twin arches of the porch yawning blackly, the one steeple caught in a ray of diffused light. The steeple? But that would have been searched long ago. She began to hurry, disturbed by her train of thought and of the doubts incurred, then tripped over something that lay concealed and fell, crying out, her hand coming into contact with slime and softness.

'Dear me,' Kenith said ruefully, hauling her to her feet and brushing the dead leaves from her breast and shoulders. 'Didn't you see that fallen tree?'

'Of course I did not!'

'Aren't you going to thank me for rescuing you?'

'I could have picked myself up.'

'I think Peter Rutherford – or Crichton – might have had a very different reception.'

'They did not come armed with a bottle and glasses with designs upon my – '

'Go on, say it. That dreaded word. Virginity.'

They stared at one another for an eternity, she angry, he intent, then, to her horror, she began to cry, not noisy bawling, but slow, silent tears that welled up and ran down her face and could not be stopped. He leaned towards her very gently and kissed her. 'You taste of salt,' he observed. 'And I was right, wasn't I? You did have regrets.'

She stood in his arms, quite still and lifeless, curiously comforted.

'You've had a bad day. Did you think you'd fallen over her?' he asked at last. 'Eleanor?'

'Yes.'

'But she can't be everywhere. I think you're still in a state of shock and should have stayed in bed.'

What he said was sensible but she had begun to react against it and his new thoughtfulness.

'Let me go.'

'Better now?'

'Much. Why aren't you taking pictures?' She tucked a curl under her bonnet brim.

'Everything's so disorganized. But like you, I'm not allowed to leave. I haven't finished, of course. Not by any means.'

'You should spend more time on your job and less womanizing.'

He laughed. 'What a lovely old-fashioned word!' Then, sobering, he told her, 'I'm not a marrying man, my dear Abigail, so it's as well that you recognize the fact. Never could abide being shackled.'

'Who's asking?' The comfort had receded as the full import of his words asserted itself. 'I've the measure of you, so never fear that I'll be under a misapprehension. The minute I saw that champagne behind your back, the scales fell from my eyes. You needn't worry. I'll expect nothing honourable.'

'I wondered when you'd mention that. Honour.'

'I suppose that's another word you despise. I do hope they find Mrs Rutherford soon. The strain of not being able to go home will be more than I can endure before long. Please keep out of my way until we are dismissed from Duncraw.'

'If that's what you really want.' He stopped short, the smile gone.

'That's what I want more than anything.'

'Very well. You do not object if I appear for meals?' he asked mock-humbly.

Abigail did not answer. She had walked some distance, very rapidly, when she discovered he was no longer there. She had not told him of that odd conversation between Geoffrey and his mother but it was none of Martin's business. She was not even sure she could tell the Inspector.

Aware of the shadowy Pringle forms with their slow, painstaking quartering of the gardens she went purposefully towards the main gate which was open. There was a Pringle on duty there and as she approached the man stepped forward. 'Sir Humphrey expects you to stay in the grounds, miss.'

'Why?'

'Because there's a woman missing.'

She opened her cloak defiantly. 'Well, do you see her hidden about my person? I cannot go far on foot. That's why I made no attempt to fetch a horse today. But I'll not be restrained like a disobedient child. And you can tell that to Sir Humphrey.'

His look of surprise as she swept past him restored her to a better humour. 'Miss!'

She ignored the summons, picking her way through the rough grass that grew up to the wall. Diffused light struck through the tall trees with their scents of resin and other, indefinable fragrances. The wind had died considerably, though branches and grasses still tossed. She enjoyed the current of air against her face and the sensation of battling against its buoyancy. A sparrowhawk floated on the breeze, its wings unmoving, quartering the ground from the sky as the Pringles did below. Perhaps that sharp yellow eye could already see what they looked for, and on the thought, the hawk dived like a stone and was lost in the complexity of bushes and blooms.

Abigail increased her pace. The gate-man had made no attempt to follow her as yet and she wanted to be out of sight when somebody did. She'd been regarded with suspicion by Peter Rutherford, and, being a comparative stranger to the house, the Inspector could view her with the same caution.

She reached the end of the wall and was confronted by the meandering progress of the stream. Looking back, she saw that another wall ran off at a right angle from the first. A short way along a gateway had been filled in with stone blocks, a relic perhaps of the aftermath of the hanging at the peel. It certainly bore out her theory that the first thing the Scotts would do would be to bar the easy entry of Crichtons. A little farther out there were distinct traces of opencast mining. The untidy mounds of weed-grown earth certainly pointed to digging for coal close to the surface. She continued her rapid walk until she saw the dark outlines of the peel rising from the dun-coloured moor. As it grew larger, she recalled that first visit, Crichton's face at the window, Charity's disappearance inside the crumbling structure, the embrace that followed the ascent of the dank staircase. Her own ridiculous sense of betrayal.

The tower had once been Scott property. It was not far from Duncraw. Why should not this have been the source of a passage to the house? Close to Cauldshiel, yet outside the walls of the Scott estate, it seemed the perfect answer.

'Miss Menory,' she said out loud. 'You have an over-active imagination.'

It occurred to her that this would be the perfect opportunity for an exploration, but the sight of two riders in the distance, who were making unmistakably in this direction, restored her to caution. They were, on closer inspection, the same two Youngs who had flanked her on the first visit to Cauldshiel.

'I've come to see Mr Crichton,' she told them, 'and you can do nothing to keep me away. I'll scream my head off if necessary.'

'No need for that, miss. He said to let you come whenever you wished. The ground's damp. You'd best take the horse and John can bring it back for me.'

'Thank you. I confess I'd not expected such civility.'

'As a matter of fact,' said the taller of the two as she was helped into the saddle, 'Mr Colin hoped you might be back today.'

They trotted in the direction of the building that looked, to her bemused gaze, more cowering and ramshackle than ever. 'Did he indeed? Was there any particular reason?' It warmed her that he had expressed such a wish.

'I think he'd prefer to tell you himself, miss.'

The sense of pleasure increased. After the difficulties of the last two days, it was encouraging that one person at least desired her presence. But no one had mentioned Charity. Since the reading of that note – in handwriting that was not wholly Charity's – she had had no contact with her friend.

She was shown into the same shabby room and asked to wait. The contents of the shelf were different. The book with the olive-green binding was no longer there. The sun had gone and the views were diffused, the vagueness of the outside world lending the occasion a spice of danger. It seemed the wind had dropped completely for nothing stirred.

She swung round to find Crichton there. 'Good morning, Miss Menory.'

'Is it – still morning?' Abigail was astonished. Her gaze lingered on the strong column of his neck, the smooth brown skin under the open neck of his shirt. He exuded animal attraction from the set of his mouth to the disordered curls. She could not blame

Charity for going to this man. If this was what she had done – her alarm grew.

'Just,' Crichton replied, smiling. A brown hand went up to fasten the shirt. The other ran over the rumpled hair in an effort to restrain it, but without noticeable effect. 'If I had known you were coming, I should have taken more pains with my appearance.'

'Why ever should you?' Her laughter was brittle. 'It's not me you must impress.'

'I was not trying to impress anyone. It was for my own satisfaction. I've been busy about the estate.'

'It does need a great deal of attention,' she agreed. 'Does your hospitality run to another dish of tea, Mr Crichton?'

'If you wish. I'd prefer whisky, myself. Could you bring yourself to join me?' His expression had lost some of its friendliness. 'I think Bessie is otherwise occupied.'

'I think I might. I've already drunk brandy this morning, why not whisky? But you'd better water it down if I've to walk back sober.'

'Brandy? Why did you need that?'

'Don't you already know?' she countered, watching him carefully.

'Know what?'

'That the disliked Mrs Rutherford is no more.'

His eyes flickered then went blank. 'Do you mean what I think?'

'Oh, come,' Abigail said. 'Let's not play games. I think it comes as no surprise.'

He was pouring whisky from a decanter that must be the most valuable thing in the room. The brown hand held out a glass quite steadily. 'Why should I know what goes on at Duncraw?'

'Why indeed? I have come to insist upon seeing Charity.' She drank to give herself courage.

'That woman. What happened?' He ignored the reference to Scott's daughter.

'She was found dead in her bed early this morning –'

'But – how? What cause?' She could almost swear his curiosity was not feigned.

'No one knows for she vanished soon after –'

Crichton took a great swig of his liquor and put back his handsome head to laugh heartily. 'You tread the realms of fantasy, Miss Menory! Mrs Rutherford must have more sense than I gave her credit for if she's run away from Scott.'

'It must remove a load from your mind that she's no longer a threat.'

'A threat!'

'She was younger than Sir Humphrey. Not altogether past child-bearing.'

Crichton finished his drink and pushed away the glass. 'My dear girl,' he said lazily, 'I think you have too little to occupy yourself. Scott's bride can have no interest for me. And ordinarily I would consider it very presumptuous of you to browbeat me in such fashion, but I recognize, lurking in the depths of all that aggression, a very real concern for Charity –'

'Where is she?'

'Why should I tell you? You've a foot in both camps. I could not entirely trust you. But this tale of Mrs Eleanor. You're not serious?'

'Quite serious. She went to sleep in that abominable Peacock Room –'

'The Peacock Bed?' His voice was now sharp.

'Yes. And though I saw her for long enough to be reasonably certain she was dead, when I took Sir Humphrey upstairs the bed was empty.'

'Tell me the whole thing from the beginning.'

She sketched the outline of the discovery and the disappearance. Crichton's eyes gleamed. They were a greenish grey, she discovered, with little flecks of yellow if one looked closely. As she spoke, he drummed his fingers on the arm of the old chair in which he sprawled, looking not unlike a clothed statue from some Greek or Roman temple, into which someone had breathed life.

He was silent when the halting recital was ended. Picking up a pen from the table, he began to tap it against his teeth in an abstracted fashion.

'I should also tell you that you may expect a call from Mr Geoffrey.'

Crichton stared. 'May I ask why?'

'Sir Humphrey decided to ignore the matter of Charity's defection but Geoffrey, besides having no expectations, seems to love Charity and wants her back.'

'Does he, by Jove! I must barricade myself in –'

'Don't joke. I feel sorry for him. It must have cost him an effort to do anything so decisive. Or even to contemplate it –'

'Contemplation's as far as young Geoff Ward is likely to get. Faith must be congratulating herself on Mrs Rutherford's demise.'

Crichton, it appeared, was more conversant with matters at Duncraw than he would have Abigail believe.

'I should not be too sure that Geoffrey will not turn up.'

'My dear Abigail, I'm not going to crumble at the thought of Charity's cousin riding up like St George to rescue her from the dragon.'

'He may do something stupid. Like coming – armed? There is the gun-room.'

'As determined as that, is he?' Surprise showed in his tone.

'He's found enough courage to turn against his mother. And he did mention force.'

'Well, well!'

'Your man said you hoped I'd be back today. Why was that?' Abigail asked.

Crichton stopped fiddling with the pen and rose to his feet to pace the uneven floor. Then he returned to stare at her fully. 'There was a pressing matter,' he said eventually and his eyes betrayed excitement. 'But it might not interest you.'

'How shall I know,' she replied, thrusting down the tendency to breathlessness, 'unless you enlighten me?'

'How indeed?'

He told her what he required of her in the gathering gloom of the darkening day.

She was half-way back when the rain came. It had threatened to fall these two hours and she was drenched in a matter of moments. The downpour went almost unnoticed. She knew now where Crichton's emotions were centred and that in itself was almost a relief. But she was not so sure about his reaction to the mystery of Eleanor Rutherford. He could be as poker-faced as the next man when it suited him.

The tower grew out of the rainswept blur. There was no one to see what she did and she'd missed luncheon so there was no point in hurrying. The bread and cheese she'd shared with Crichton would last until dinner this evening. It would be somewhere to shelter until the rain stopped, she told herself. But it was also a place that might reward an investigation.

Hurrying up the dripping steps, she found herself in a small square room in which two narrow slits let in the minimum of light. The walls, of big, uneven stones, between which rough cement had been used in a fruitless effort to hold the place together, contained only one other intended opening, that of a fireplace, above which, by dint of much stretching, she could see the grey sky at the end of a long vent. Raindrops fell into her eyes and she withdrew hastily. The places where stones had become dislodged disclosed no secret openings.

Biting her lip, she went up the inside stair. It was narrow and the edges of the steps were worn and dangerous. The walls were in better condition, but rubbed against her skin like emery paper. Her wet boot slid off one of the eroded edges and she clung to the rough surface, her heart thudding, until she recovered her balance. Voluminous skirts were not for such deathtraps, particularly when sodden with water.

The room above was a facsimile of the one downstairs except that it was in better condition. It had been a waste of time coming up for, logically, a hidden passage must go under the building. Remembering the steps by which one entered, she realized there must be a space beneath the tower for the floor was level with the entrance from which the door had long since rotted. She came down again carefully, holding up the uncomfortably heavy material and feeling for each step with exaggerated caution. The rain still swept against the sides of the peel with cold ferocity.

Something ran across the rough floor as she regained the original chamber. It was almost certainly a rat, she decided, shuddering. The chamber seemed not so dark and she could see the thick coating of dust and the myriad lumps of stone that covered the floor, concealing it from all but casual view. Rain had begun to penetrate the openings and runnels of water combined with the powdery muck. It was all very cheerless. The warming effect of the whisky was dissipating and her clothes felt chilly and constricting. But she walked about, pushing aside the smaller stones with the toe of her boot, lifting away the larger ones in an endeavour to find a trace of some trapdoor or loosened flagstone that could lead underground. There was nothing.

But it did not need to be up here. With a mounting turbulence, she made for the gap of the doorway and began the slippery descent, but the mud from the chamber had covered one boot sole and she slipped on the second step, crashing all the way down to fall with her back slammed against the wall and the breath gone from her body. She did not dare move. Her whole body ached miserably and her backbone felt raw.

Slowly, her breathing became more even. She groaned a little, then moved each leg in turn. They did not seem broken but her left arm and shoulder were shot through with pain. She stretched out the injured arm and her hand came into contact with something small and metallic that lay in the tufted grass. Wincing, she pushed it out into the open. It was a snuff-box, silver, engraved with curling initials. K.M.

Abigail looked at it for an age in the soft, driving rain, barely conscious of the myriad small cuts and abrasions in the greater hurt of her bruised shoulder. It could only belong to one person. Kenith Martin had been here. But why? He could never have hauled all that heavy apparatus to the tower unnoticed. And why else should a photographer have wanted to visit the place? He had admitted to a besetting curiosity but instinct told her he must have some other purpose. Had he come, as she had, to look for some secret way? Or had he used it before Eleanor's death?

She pushed herself to her feet then bent, groaning, to pick up the box with her good hand and slipped it into a pocket. She moved the impaired arm and tried to flex the fingers but the fall was too recent. It was nothing, of course, that would not respond to a really hot bath, and she would certainly not go until she had circumvented the base of the tower. Shaken she might be, but the weather could not do any more damage than she had already suffered. Forcing her weary body along, she shuffled around the peel, stumbling among the tussocks. Then, shivering, she began to descend the rough track to the now-swollen stream.

There was someone coming along the road and that someone was in a hurry. Caught on the first of the stepping-stones, her body stiff with bruises, she could not conceal herself. But she forced herself on in an effort to be, at least, on the right side of the water. It was a vain attempt for she was only halfway across when Geoffrey came into sight, his heels digging into the flanks of a sweating horse.

He pulled up suddenly. 'Have you fallen in the stream? Whatever are you doing down there?'

'I was caught in the rain. Trespassing, I'm afraid – and hoping someone would rescue me and take me back to the house. I fell down some steps and that is why I look so – so disorderly. Help me – please.'

'You might have broken something or lain out there for long enough and caught pneumonia.'

'I might. But I didn't. I have a sore shoulder and a numb wrist and that is all. But I am so wet I could take a chill if I do not get into a mustard bath immediately. You will take me back to the house?'

She stood there, muddy, pathetic, the feather in her bonnet heavy with moisture, her hair bedraggled. He dismounted reluctantly and came towards her, holding out an arm.

'I was – ' he said with an effort, 'going elsewhere.'

'Then have second thoughts. He'd be too strong for you, Mr Ward. I know.'

'I did not say – '

'There was no need.' He had hold of her wrist and had swung her over to stand beside him.

'But Charity – '

'Would not have you willingly even if Crichton did not exist. Which he does. And what's more, he has all the Youngs behind him. A very tough young man. Would you want Charity, knowing that she'd flinch from your every touch?'

Geoffrey released her so suddenly that she slithered backwards. Just in time he seized her and pulled her back to face him. 'You know that what I say is true, don't you?' she said gently.

His face whitened. 'Then it has all been for nothing.'

Abigail stared, not daring to ask him what he meant, but determined to push her advantage. 'It was not her doing, the engagement. It was all his. Charity was never considered. A hard man, Sir Humphrey – '

'I hate him,' Geoffrey said, 'Then you think – ?'

'It would be useless to go banging at the door of Cauldshiel. Crichton would be expecting you. You could not surprise him. And even if you were armed, he'd anticipate that too. You are, are you not? You would only store up trouble you could never solve.'

His hand slid to his thigh. 'You know a deal too much, Miss Abigail. But I'll think over what you said. I won't say I'll take your advice in the long run because I do not know.' He shrugged. 'You'd best come and share my horse. He's big enough for us both.'

'Has anything happened in my absence?' she asked as they began to travel alongside the pink wall, the trees a wet blur, her body jolting hurtfully.

'Peter Rutherford has taken to his room.'

'I am not surprised. She has not been found?'

'Not a sign.'

'And Sir Humphrey?'

'I've kept out of his way. Understandably.' Again the bitterness crept through.

'So, nothing has really changed.'

'The servants are disorganized. First the house is searched for missing valuables. Now it is searched again for a body. They are all agog, their previous annoyance turned to a variety of reactions. Some with the vapours, some devoured with excitement. More enjoy sensation, I fear, than are rational.'

'It is always the same when routine is disrupted. And you must admit, the circumstances were most dramatic.'

'I suppose so.' For the first time his voice was guarded. 'But it was quite opportune that an Inspector of Police should be in the house.'

'I had almost forgotten. I thought I heard voices in the Peacock Room the night of my arrival.'

'Did you tell anyone?' His arm tightened round her involuntarily.

'Only Charity.'

'Why not the Inspector?'

'It went out of my head when I found Mrs Rutherford. But I'm convinced now there must be some sort of entrance to that room.'

'Are you? I've never heard of one. Neither has Mother.'

'It could be the sort of thing only the Master of the House is told. Passed from father to son like the location of the secret room in the Castle of Glamis.'

'What do you know of that?'

'My father had a friend who was a guest there. The secret was never divulged till the son's coming of age.'

'I see.' They were almost back at the gate and Abigail could see the figure of the Pringle guard, the rain dripping from his cape and hard hat, the butt of the rifle.

'Then why has Sir Humphrey not mentioned it?' Geoffrey shrugged.

'Because – how old was he when his father died?' Abigail asked, aware of the cold Pringle gaze as they turned into the drive.

'He must have been quite young. Sir John was killed at Waterloo.'

'So, Sir Humphrey must have been four or five at the most. Certainly not of age.'

'But surely he'd make some provision – Sir John? For passing on the secret?'

'He probably thought he was indestructible. A large number of people imagine themselves to be. If he was a good soldier he'd expect to come back. And he must have been young.'

'It's only a theory,' Geoffrey objected. 'Perhaps Sir Humphrey *does* know. And only chose to say nothing! But why – ?' His question petered out on a renewal of the downpour. The green archway of the beeches dripped monotonously.

Abigail did not reply. If Geoffrey was right there could only be one answer.

* * *

Jeannie clucked like a hen over one chick when she saw Abigail. 'Get them wet things off, miss!' she exclaimed, scandalized. 'A hot bath's what you need,' and half an hour later, Abigail sat in the painted tub, while the maid took away the heap of sodden clothing. Every stitch she had worn required attention. The hot water and liberal addition of mustard was working miracles on her sore body.

Gloriously warm, she wrapped herself in a large towel while Jeannie took out fresh, dry clothes and helped her to dress. 'Imagine slipping and hurting your arm!'

'I was not to know it would rain, or that the ground would turn to a quagmire.'

'I suppose not. Would you like it if I kept you company tonight, Miss Abigail? It couldn't have been very nice for you this morning and these rooms can be quite creepy after dark. All those empty ones. Thinking you hear something. There's a little bed we could put in the corner if I moved the small chest.'

'Oh, Jeannie! Would you? I was longing to ask. But it seemed so pathetic. I'm used to being independent and I find I'm not even capable of sustaining that under duress.'

'I'll shift the things while you are at dinner.'

'Will there be the usual meal?' Abigail arranged her lace collar and began to brush her drying hair. The red strands made crackling noises as they were smoothed into a semblance of order but the little neck curls were as unruly as ever. She looked much too feminine this evening.

'Oh, yes. Far more sensible than everyone having trays like Mr Peter.'

'He must be very upset.'

'He is. When Molly took his food, she saw some pills lying on the little table. And he had the screen drawn across the side of the fireplace as though he couldn't warm himself properly, and a good fire going too. Strange, he looked.'

'How disturbing.'

'He took the tray at the door and mumbled he wouldn't want to be disturbed any more unless there was word of his mother. And Molly swears she heard the sound of a decanter – the clink of the stopper – just as she set off again. *And* the key turn.'

'A doctor should know that drugs and drink are not good.'

'But there's no denying there's much he has to forget.'

'Yes, Jeannie. Will – everyone else be at dinner?'

'Don't rightly know about Miss Hope. No one ever could count on that girl. But there'll be the rest of them. Sir Humphrey always keeps up appearances and Mrs Ward will be lording it in her old place. She'd not miss that.'

Faith must be in her element. Even though Charity had disappointed Geoffrey her own position seemed secure.

She was last to enter the long, atmospheric room. The candle flames burned high, reflecting themselves in the prisms of the chandelier. Faith had had the tact or good sense not to sit where Mrs Rutherford had been the previous night. Impossible to believe she had been there yesterday.

Sir Humphrey looked hunched and curiously diminished. Already his glass was filled and he drank from it, cradling the fine crystal as though for comfort. Geoffrey, very straight-backed, stared at the cloth. The Inspector watched Abigail approach, a frown between his sandy brows. Kenith Martin had a queer little smile on his lips, an impeccable cravat and an elegant black coat in place of last night's grey. Unhappiness attacked her. He had said so definitely that marriage had no place in his life. And she could never be anyone's mistress for all her reasonably advanced ideas. She needed permanence, a wholehearted commitment.

Faith and Sir Humphrey had begun a lack-lustre conversation to which the Inspector listened in a desultory fashion.

'Do you feel better?' Geoffrey asked Abigail.

'Much, thank you.' He had not looked at her and she had the curious feeling that he had shut himself into some secret compartment where no one could reach him.

'You look very pretty this evening,' Martin told her softly. He had the facility of being able to hold an almost inaudible conversation that still managed to emblazon itself on her mind like a bright banner. 'Not as you did an hour or two back. A very bedraggled little hen, that was. But certainly not bowed. A triumphant tilt to the head, I thought.'

'I swear you see everything.' She noticed for the first time that Hope was absent.

'My weakness. I told you.'

'But you don't see enough to unravel the great mystery?'

'I am not God.'

'I found something I think must be yours.'

'I do not remember losing anything.' Had his smile grown a little more fixed?

'I cannot think of anyone else with the initials K.M.'

'Initials?' Martin felt in all his pockets then turned on her a gaze that was full of innocence. 'My snuffbox! I did miss it but I thought, with changes of clothing, I had left it in another coat. I'm sure I must have. How did you get it? And where?'

Conscious of Hod at her elbow with a soup tureen, she remained quiet until he had moved away. Then, opening the reticule, she took out the little silver box and passed it to Kenith under cover of the table. The long, dark fingers closed over it. 'It – is mine.'

'I've never seen you use snuff.'

'I never have. The box belonged to my father. It's very small, as you may have noticed. No trouble to carry with me. It has sentimental associations.'

'And yet you lose it in long grass in a place where it might never have been seen again?'

'And where might that have been, Miss Menory?'

She took some soup, wishing, cruelly, to prolong his suspense. Not liking herself for the cat-and-mouse tactics, she said, 'Do you really not know?'

'I swear it.'

'Well, then, at –' her voice dropped – 'the Hanging Tower.'

'So that's where you've been! And not for the first time.' Then, noticing Sir Humphrey's growing attention, he went on quietly, 'There was nothing, was there? Not the sort of thing that might have interested you.'

'But, when – ?'

'I did not go the orthodox way. The gate's too public. And I had to see it in daylight.'

'Then – the wall?'

'Skilfully evading Pringles to right and to left, I made my athletic escape. It was you inspired me.'

'When did you go?'

'While you and Charity went to Hawick. It did not take long and the day was fine, if you remember.'

'Yes. I remember.' The recollection was tinged with sadness.

'You made it sound something not to be missed, and I am interested in photography. Only I could not see how I could get close enough without trespassing.'

'But you *did* trespass. I found it by the wall.'

'Close enough with my paraphernalia, I meant. As if you did not know.'

'That could present difficulties.'

Hod was back with potatoes while a footman gathered the soup-plates.

'It's a pity,' Abigail said, 'that you'll not be able to do as your father did.'

'And what is that?' Martin asked, frowning.

'Pass on the snuff-box to your son.'

Silence descended on the dinner table.

As they rose to leave, Martin said, 'I do actually have your picture now.'

Abigail coloured. 'That old story!'

'That now true story,' he said reprovingly.

'You need not ask to come to my room. Once bitten.'

'There's nothing shy about you. So don't pretend. Oh, and by the way, you may chalk up a victory.'

'Victory?' The candles had burned down and were beginning to smoke.

'That rather cutting observation about the snuff-box. But how do you know that I have not already a son?' His shadow was large upon the wall.

'I confess I know nothing about you. But, if you have, you cannot think much of the child.'

'And why not?'

'To withhold from him your own name.'

'Perhaps he already has my name.'

'Then – you *are* married? I thought – you objected to the state.' The chill after the candlelit warmth of the dining-room struck cold upon her neck and shoulders.

'I was married.' His tone was sombre. 'We were neither of us happy after a time. She died.'

'And you really have a child?'

'A boy. My sister has care of him. Little James –'

'If I had known, I should never have said what I did.'

'I know that. I should like you to see the picture.'

'I – I will go to the withdrawing-room. No one goes there much as a rule.'

'Very well. I'll fetch it.'

She went to the withdrawing-room and sat by the fire. At first it did not seem so bad that his unwillingness to marry was the result of an unhappy relationship. But then she remembered that he had insinuated they were happy at the beginning, he and his dead wife. He'd never bring himself to taste that particular cake a second time for fear the same thing happened. The knowledge of his closeness to another woman was unexpectedly wounding. She conjured up the face of his child, dark and Stuart as his own, and thought that she could love it. But what if it resembled her? The shadow of a past wife could prove stronger than that of a present lover. Johanne had proved that. Her influence still lay over this house, over child and husband alike.

Abigail wound her arms around her knees and tried not to think of Martin and the life in which she'd had no part, of loving and hating and a child born in wretchedness. She found herself sorry for the boy who seemed virtually parentless. But it was none of her business. Martin had warned her there was no futurity in becoming involved with himself and now he'd elaborated on the discouragement.

She looked up as someone entered the room but it was not Martin as she had expected. Sir Humphrey faced her, shorn of arrogance and mystique. He was a rather pathetic middle-aged man beset by difficulties he resented and did not understand.

'I must ask you,' he said without preamble, 'why you mentioned Hope? This is my daughter's home and just the sight of her last night could not have seemed unusual without something added, something suspicious. What was it, Miss Menory?'

'She was carrying a cup.' She'd known all along the time must come to say it.

'What is so odd about that?'

'Mrs Rutherford looked so untouched. As though she might have taken some draught.'

'I see.'

'If she had suffered some stroke or convulsion, it would have shown in her expression. I had an aunt who suffered one and Mrs Rutherford looked quite different.'

'And Eleanor appeared – peaceful?'

'Quite.'

'I'm glad of that. But did it not occur to you that the last thing Hope would have done was to offer any kindness to a prospective stepmother?'

'Unless she was making an effort to reconcile herself to the situation. Perhaps she had thought the matter over and was afraid of losing you entirely. You did seem set on your course of action.'

'No, Miss Menory. The cup would be for herself. I know you probably meant to be kind when you explained your theory to the Inspector but that is the true explanation of Hope's presence near the Peacock Room. Did you – did you mention the cup? To anyone but me, that is?'

'No.'

'Well, I beg you will not.'

'As you begged me not to mention the contents of your study cupboard?'

'I am making use of your goodwill. But, believe me, there are good reasons.'

'I'm sure there must be. Sir Humphrey, Mrs. Rutherford *must* be in the house.'

'She is not.'

'Well, then, her body has been removed via some secret way? Like Felicity Croser's? In which case we need look no farther than the room where they were last seen.'

Sir Humphrey looked wearily cynical. 'A theory previously expounded but so far not upheld.'

'Then you do not know of it?'

'No. If my father was aware of any such exit, he kept it to himself.'

'And – the Pringles?'

'Rest assured that if they knew, then so would I.'

'Yes. I imagined that would be the position.' Abigail was thoughtful. 'Then why did I imagine I heard voices coming from there on my first night here?'

'They could have been coming from the floor below. There are several places in the house where sounds rise more clearly. Spaces between ceiling and joists – changes through the years.'

'Then, which room is below the Peacock Room?'

'Mr Martin's and the Inspector's is next door, under yours.'

'But Mr Martin was not here at the time. I saw his very ostentatious arrival the following day, *and* he picked up the Inspector whose horse had the unfortunate misfortune to become lame just at the foot of the drive. Neither was then installed at Duncraw.'

'But the servants had to prepare the rooms. Knowing them, they'd not do it silently.'

'Not even with Mrs Davison there?'

'She cannot be there all the time. I doubt she would be at night.'

165

'I suppose not. Then I must have been mistaken.'

'I'm afraid you must.' Sir Humphrey rose from the same white-covered chair that had been Charity's favourite. Abigail had a vivid picture of her seated there with her golden hair spread out over the velvet cushion. The geranium red was as kind to the laird's greying head as it had been to Charity's.

'Sir Humphrey, could you not find it in your heart to forgive your daughter? For being the cause of her mother's death. She has suffered enough, don't you think?'

'We have all suffered, Miss Menory.' His lips clamped together as though he could never open them again in friendship. The old martinet look had returned.

'Sir Humphrey—' But he shook his head a little blindly and went out of the room.

Martin appeared with suspicious alacrity. 'What did he want?'

'I suspect you know already, though you'd never admit it.'

'No one ever admits to curiosity. It's always kept decently in check, behind lace curtains if necessary. Some friends of mine were passing a spinster's house, well known for her avid compulsion to know everything, when her curtains fell about her ears—'

Abigail snorted with laughter. 'Really! You are quite impossible.'

'But it's true. She strained so hard to see what they were doing, the accident was unavoidable. That's what happens to frustrated women. They are forced to live through others.'

'And what happens to frustrated men?'

'I cannot describe their tortures.' Something in his voice quelled the desire to laugh.

'Let me see the picture.'

He held it out silently. It was very good, Abigail thought. In fact, it was better than good. It was superlative. He really had a supreme gift of getting the best out of his subject. Any thoughts she had entertained about him playing at photography were stilled. At exactly the right moment, the shutter had clicked on impeccable lighting, on the hint of a smile that was so much more subtle than a full-blooded grin, on a mixture of light and shade that made this piece of pasteboard a thing of beauty. Against the softness of her body, the luminosity of her skin, the carving took on an extra dimension and solidity, each intricacy meshed into a beguiling chiaroscuro.

'You like it?'

She raised her eyes to meet his. 'How could I do otherwise? You're – a genius.'

'Only lucky. I'm a dabbler, really – '

'Do not pretend. You're an artist. You have to be. It's worth a good fee.'

He looked displeased. 'It was not done for that reason!'

'But I'm a very independent woman. I like to pay for what I receive.'

'Then you can.' It was perfectly plain what he meant.

Her smile faded. 'I had not realized you'd be so persistent. I find it a matter for pity that you must seek for hole-and-corner affairs because one woman has disappointed you. Not everyone brings disaster. My parents had something precious that was only lost with their dying. Sir Humphrey and his wife Johanne – '

'Had something that should have ended with her death – '

'How can you say that?'

'You did not allow me to finish. I was going to say, more properly, that should have changed with her death and not become a monster to haunt a whole family. You know I am right.'

She said nothing. It was true. The picture she held blurred then became clear again.

'I find, Miss Menory, that I cannot do without you,' Martin was saying, 'and so, I am asking you to marry me.'

Abigail, roused from pity for the Scotts, said sharply, 'If you think that you can avail yourself of me – and I still cannot fathom what you see in me – merely by a promise of marriage you will conveniently forget the following morning, you are sadly mistaken.'

'But, Abigail – '

'In any case,' she said austerely, 'I have other plans.'

'Other plans?' His surprise amused her.

'Strange as it may seem, yes.'

She left him staring after her with a kind of anger.

SEVEN

Jeannie's temporary bed had been installed during dinner, and its presence, with the promise of the girl's physical proximity, cheered Abigail. She had been close to tears on her hurried ascent of the stairs. It had been hard to take a strong line with Martin, and once it had been done the echoes of his voice returned to her like the insinuations of the Devil.

The shadow of Eleanor's disappearance still lay over the house. Abigail had found herself, like the maid, Molly, hesitating outside Peter's door, but before she had heard anything she remembered what Martin had said about frustrated spinsters and lace curtains and she'd almost run from the spot, her cheeks flaming. He had not meant the proposal to be taken seriously. It was merely a way to soften her. Discovering she still held the photograph, she realized she'd meant to give it back but had been so taken aback by his whispered confession. 'Cannot do without you,' well, he'd have to do without her!

She did have other plans that involved Crichton, but they were no one's business but her own. Abigail supposed they'd give her a pleasure of sorts.

The photograph drew her again with its depth of light and shade, the nuances of skin tone and fabric, wood and plaster. Martin need never be out of work if he could produce such effects consistently. There was only one small blemish, a tiny dark patch on the carved wall – she stared at it intently.

'Am I too early, miss?' Jeannie was at the door, her plain face overlaid with an expression of keenest anticipation. 'Mrs Davison said it would be all right.'

Abigail started and almost dropped the pictured likeness. Rising, she put it on the mantel. 'You aren't too early. I feel rather foolish to tell the truth!'

'I do not think you are. None of us do. I'd not want to be up here alone. There's no one else on the floor.'

'But there's no legend attached to this room, so neither of us need be nervous.'

'No.'

Jeannie had turned her back to divest herself of the black gown, to reveal sturdy shoulders and strong, coarse under-garments. Abigail looked away discreetly. She wanted to talk, to fill in the time between now and sleeping.

'A real good picture Mr Martin took there. Hardly know it was you, though, Miss Abigail. What did he say to you to make you look like that?'

'I don't remember.' She did, of course, only too well.

'He's a funny gentleman. Took all the staff, he did, though it wasn't easy, most of them laughing at first, or fidgeting. Threatened us all with head clamps, he did, and that sobered everybody double quick. Put us in rows, some standing, some sitting, with Mrs Davison and Hod in the middle.'

'All Pringles,' Abigail could not resist saying.

'There've always been Pringles at Duncraw.'

'I know.'

'And none the worse for that for all that woman said the things she did!'

'I agree. A fine body of men.'

'*And* women.' Martin would have appreciated that,

Abigail thought, with a twist of half pain, half secret laughter.

'Of course, and women,' she made herself say gravely.

'Funny to think,' Jeannie said, when they were both stretched out in their respective beds, 'that she's lying somewhere around. Mrs Rutherford.' The woman did indeed seem to dominate the place as much dead as alive. Abigail realized she had to accept the fact until either the topic faded with time or was accentuated by the delicious horror of discovery.

'Where else might one hide corpses?' she asked, half-jokingly. 'Ditches? An old well?'

'Oh, miss!' Jeannie shot up in bed, causing the candle-flame to turn almost horizontal. 'There *is* an old well! It ran dry when the river changed course and other one was sunk. The old one's all hidden with weeds and brambles now and no one goes there. Just the sort of place a murderer might think of –'

'If he knew of its existence,' Abigail reminded her, glad that the candle had not been blown out. She lay back, silent, only dimly hearing Jeannie's chattering voice.

The pain in her shoulder nibbled at the nerve-ends like a rat.

'Good night, Jeannie,' she said, knowing she would not close her eyes for a long time.

'Good night,' Jeannie said and yawned comfortably. The bed creaked as she turned on her side, face to the wall. Soon, her regular breathing indicated she was asleep.

The candle burned lower but still Abigail lay wakeful. Jeannie's form, hidden as it was by a white counterpane, looked horribly still. Even the dark was better than looking at such immobility. Abigail snuffed out the small flame.

* * *

The well was not easy to find. Running the gauntlet of indirect Pringle stares, Abigail made her escape after an uneasy breakfast attended by everyone except Peter Rutherford.

The sun was shining again and the unseasonal cold nip had gone out of the air. No one wanted Abigail and yet she could not simply pack her things ready for departure. One of the Pringles had been despatched on a mysterious errand but no one else was allowed to leave. The Inspector was firm on that point. He had gained assurance in the last few days.

'I can walk in the grounds?' she asked. 'I begin to feel a prisoner.'

'So long as I know where you are.'

'I will take a turn in the fresh air. It will help to pass the time.'

'You do not think you'd be well advised to take a companion?'

She shrugged. 'Who should I take? The servants are about their business. No one wants my company.'

'Disturbing things have happened. Could still happen –'

'Then I will have to take that chance. I can stay confined no longer.'

'But take care,' he insisted, and for once the sandy hair was tidy.

'Where will you be if I should scream?' she asked, teasing.

'Do not joke, Miss Menory.'

His portentous expression made her laugh. 'I will scream into the wind,' she said almost gaily. 'Then it will be carried in your direction.'

He pushed in his chin disapprovingly.

'No one can have any reason for harming me,' she went on more soberly.

'How can you know that? I can tell you, more than

one has – ' He stopped maddeningly, inflaming her curiosity.

'You're a sadist, Inspector Moray,' she accused.

'You almost made me indiscreet,' he said and ruffled his thick hair into its accustomed tangle. She preferred him that way, she decided, watching, with regret, his determined departure. If only he had finished the sentence. But there was still the old well.

She walked the garden very decorously to begin with so that any Pringle suspicions would be allayed by the sight of her abstracted air and sedate perambulations. The disused well could not be too far from the present one, she decided, and logically it should be closer to the river since the diversion had robbed the original well of its water.

Sitting on the new well's stone edge, she stared down at the round glitter of reflection. The river, according to her recollections, lay over to the left. Between her and the outer wall of the grounds lay a desolation of thick shrubs and small trees, the tall pinkish spires of willowherb and usual bramble trails.

She moved towards the wild thicket without haste, pausing to stare up at the boughs through which the sun glinted, as though entranced by that splendour. Then, a swift tug at the mesh of branches and she was behind the leafy screen and calculating the least harmful way through the overgrown maze. Someone had been here before her. The weeds were pressed flat in places as though crushed under a heavy tread. A man who carried a body might leave such traces. Mrs Gaskell, Abigail thought, and beat down an inclination to laugh without real amusement, would be in her element.

She picked up her skirts, glad she had worn green for the colour blended with the tints of the foliage, and followed the tracks. Thorns of bramble caught at her ankles and nettles grew high. Thin, whiplash branches slapped at her face. And there were rustles that stopped when she did. Rabbits, she told herself. Small, country creatures –

She hardly believed it when she caught the glimpse of mossy stone, but, pressing forward, she saw the unmistakable outlines of eroded blocks, detached from the main ruin, concealed as Jeannie had told her, by a matted growth of weeds and ivy. Pulling away the strong grass she beat her way to the crumbled rim and leaned, panting, against the edge.

She found herself staring into the dankness of the old well. A long way below she caught a glimpse of something white.

The whiteness, she thought through waves of sickness, was about the size of a woman's face. She stared until her eyes ached. There were darknesses that could be eyesockets, an open mouth, but it was too far off to be sure.

'It's a sheep's skull,' a voice said from behind her.

She gasped, faltered and was grasped by a strong hand.

'I came to warn you it was dangerous,' Hod Pringle told her and set her on her feet as another stone rolled from the side of the structure to fall inside the well, reverberating inside the shaft.

Her lips thin and white with shock, she stared at him wordlessly.

'Been there a long time, that sheep. Nothing much round here that a Pringle don't know about.'

'How did you know I was here?'

'Saw you. I'm paid to see things. You tried too hard to look innocent, Miss Menory.'

'I did not see you.'

'Gamekeepers and the like don't let themselves be seen,' he said stolidly.

'But I heard you!' she said triumphantly, the disturbance of his appearance diminishing. 'Surely I should not have done?'

'Seems I slipped up there, miss.' He smiled unwillingly.

'Though I did think it was rabbits, or weasels,' she conceded.

'Careless of me,' he answered. 'But shifting up to the house in the main spoils the reflexes.'

He had not moved away and she was conscious of his closeness, his toughness. But if he'd intended her any harm he'd have let her fall down the well after that beastly stone.

'How do you know it's a sheep? It's a long way down.'

'Take my word for it, miss. It's nothing that's been put there recent, like, just in case that's what you're thinking.'

'Well, since you mention it, I did think –'

'That it was Mrs High and Mighty?'

'I thought it was Mrs Rutherford.'

'Same thing. We've no cause to be hypocrites, Miss Menory. Not the Pringles.'

Still, he kept her hemmed in beside the dangerous edifice. She would have to push past him to escape. 'I should like to go back to the house,' she said. 'The Inspector knows I am out here. I've already spoken to him. In fact he warned me –'

'Warned you?' A curious note had infiltrated Hod's quiet tones.

'Said I should take a companion. Disquieting events had taken place.'

'Oh. Said that, did he?' The keen gaze never wavered.

'He told me, well, as good as, that more than one person had been threatened.' Abigail knew that this was a distortion of the truth, and probably not what the Inspector had meant, but it sounded good enough to dissuade Hod from anything he could have in mind. 'I said I would scream if I felt endangered.' She pretended lightness.

'You needn't scream because of me, miss,' Hod told her, his expression unchanging. 'I saw you going somewhere that needs watching. Could have collapsed altogether, that well, when you leaned on it.'

'Well, it should be fenced off, then, shouldn't it?'

'Don't worry, miss. It shall be. Now, I think you'd best come with me.'

'I can find my own way back.'

'If the Inspector thinks there's any danger, I'd be failing in my duty if I didn't see you safely back as far as the house.' He was inflexible.

'I'll come after you, then.' Somehow, the thought of Hod behind her was too disagreeable to be borne.

'Might get a branch across your face,' he warned.

'I'll take that chance.'

'Very well.' He sounded sullen as he moved off, looking backwards to see if she was, indeed, following. Abigail took a few steps, kicking away the undergrowth that sprang back as Hod made his way. Neither spoke as the difficulties of the thicket were traversed. Abigail was flushed of face and tangled of hair when they emerged from the last of the trees. Her skirt was snagged and her stockings torn in at least one place. There was no one to blame but herself but she resented being marshalled like a disobedient child. And there was still that nagging doubt about the contents of the well. Hod was glib but how did she know he had told the truth?

They were crossing a patch of lawn when she saw

Kenith Martin appear at the end of the path that led to the stables. Hod's shadow lay on her like that of a jailer. She waved at Martin and watched him hesitate. 'You promised to show me your dark room,' she called out.

Hod was waiting. Indignation forced her to further folly. 'Can I come now? I've nothing better to do.'

'Very well,' Martin said without noticeable enthusiasm. 'But there's nothing to see.'

'Please – '

He smiled carefully. 'Come along, then.' He did not want her presence but she was determined to be free of Pringle at all costs.

The grass was soft under her feet. Abigail discovered that her arm was hurting again. Hod's grip on her had been harder than she thought.

'You refused my previous invitation,' Martin said as they proceeded towards the stable.

'Well, now I am accepting it.'

'I confess, I fail to comprehend you. You reproach me over breakfast. We have come to the understanding that you do not want me as either lover or husband. What was it you said? "I have other plans." I might have made mine.'

'Have you?'

'Not yet.'

'Well, cannot you show me all those treasures of your craft without any personal element to spoil it? If you want to know, I had had enough of Hod Pringle.'

Martin swung round displeased, his dark eyes taking in her dishevelled appearance, the obvious disorder of her skirts. 'He has not taken advantage of you?'

'Never laid a finger on me. Wait, I lie. He grabbed me by the wrist. See? There is already a bruise.'

'I have it in my mind to teach the boor a lesson he'll

not forget.' Martin sounded angry. It was extraordinary how happy she was made by his reaction.

'He was dragging me away from the disused well which I had discovered earlier.'

'Did he say why?' Martin asked after a pause.

'It was in a bad state of repair. He was probably justified. It's just that –'

'You dislike being bested.' The anger was replaced by amusement.

'Why must women be continually expected to submit?'

'Why indeed.' The amusement was intensified. How easily he could switch to charm.

'I can see you do not care!'

'Then you cannot see at all.'

The door of the stable stood open and the vast bulk of the caravan loomed in the shadows.

'I'm afraid the dark room is out of bounds. I have rigged it in the other part of the stable but it contains valuable plates I cannot afford to damage at this juncture.'

'Then show me the rest. If the Pringles are allowed, why not I?'

'Stand back then while I light this lantern. I must be careful because of the fire risk.'

She waited obediently until the warm glow steadied and Martin beckoned her from the flap of the caravan. She took the hand he offered and was pulled up beside him. In obedience to impulse she gazed at rows and rows of little tubes in wooden racks, deep metal trays, bottles out of which came smells so pungent that her eyes smarted. Enamel basins of varying sizes, the thermometers, the stove. An enormous trunk or chest of the hair variety that looked incredibly sinister, and out of which must have come some of these objects. An open ledger in which neat columns bore sets of calculations. Very much what she had expected to see, except for the hair trunk. It was big enough to hold *two* bodies, she reflected, then pushed the thought away.

'Well?' His voice stole out of the half-obscurity.

'It's – impressive. Though I can never quite believe that all this could be dragged up a mountain.'

'It was. I have seen the photographs.'

'I suppose we are all Doubting Thomases until we see the indisputable proof.'

'Human nature.'

'I am sorry if I seemed to take you to task at breakfast.'

The lantern wavered momentarily. 'Only seemed?'

'Well, I was condemnatory. For all I know, you see a good deal of your son. I confess, I really would like to see the child – ' She needed, for some reason, to know all there was to know about Martin. Before it was too late.

'Indeed?'

'As I would enjoy seeing Edinburgh before I go away. Peter Rutherford made it sound somewhere not to be missed.'

'It is beautiful. There is nowhere like it.'

'Then, couldn't we go? There must be a limit to the photographs you need take.'

'I'm sorry,' he said formally. 'But it will not be possible.' He blew out the lantern decisively. 'Let me help you to alight.'

'You blow hot and cold,' Abigail said, her feelings of rejection strong.

'And you!' he reminded sharply. 'You've other plans, or so you said. Unless that was meant to keep me dangling – as if I would – '

'Damnation!' Abigail said passionately. 'I wanted to be sure. Can't you understand?'

'It is still not possible for me to take you to Edinburgh. Not at this time.'

'Very well. Rest assured I will not ask again. I cannot think what made me do so this morning. You've at least made up my mind about one thing.' She bent down to decide the best way to descend unaided but he forestalled her by swinging himself down with great agility and seizing her by the waist to lift her from the platform of the van.

'I hope no one sees you leave here in that state,' he observed, the dark gaze roaming over her mussed hair and general appearance of disorderliness. 'I seem to recall you wanted no gossip about us but you do present the suggestion of some bucolic tumbling.'

'I detest you!' she cried, trying vainly to smooth herself into some semblance of order.

'Shakespeare had an answer to that,' he observed irritatingly. 'About too much protestation.' And he laughed.

She lifted up the now disreputable skirts and swept from the place angrily. Not only had she been caught at a disadvantage by Hod Pringle, but Martin had scored a decisive victory by his cold refusal to her suggestion they visit his home, his city. If he had meant that proposal he would have welcomed the project as a weakening of her former resolution. His offer of marriage had been, as she feared, a subterfuge to overcome her opposition to his attempts at seduction. She supposed that it was better to know that she had been right about him, but the truth was the reverse. She was cold and miserable and hated the necessity of remaining here another day.

But there was tomorrow.

She decided, next morning, to ask Sir Humphrey directly if she could take Suzy out for an hour or so.

Hod, as usual, was there, ministering to his lord and master, his grey gaze reminiscent with memories of his triumph at the well.

'I have walked the grounds until I know each bush,' she complained. 'It is not my wish to remain at Duncraw. It is yours. And I give my word of honour that I'll come back. No light promise. And my luggage remains in my room as surety. If I am required to stay, I must insist upon a little freedom.'

Sir Humphrey raised his splendid head as a stag might upon scenting a hunting party. 'May I ask where you intend to go?'

'Oh, here and there. Not far. Here I am in the way and you need not protest, Mrs Ward. You have your hands full enough. I have become an embarrassment. We do not know one another, have no ties of blood or friendship as existed between myself and Charity.'

Faith coloured faintly. 'I do not see the harm,' she began, but Scott interrupted.

'The Inspector,' he began, but was interrupted in his turn by Moray.

'I think we can respect Miss Menory's word,' he said surprisingly.

'Very well,' Scott agreed with a note of reserve. But he had sufficient to occupy him and it was unlikely he'd give her another thought once she'd gone. There were a myriad perplexing matters that remained to be cleared up.

Hope was quiet as usual. She had moped since Peter Rutherford had taken to his bed and Abigail had seen the girl near his door yesterday evening as though trying to pluck up the courage to approach him.

Geoffrey had announced his intention of going to Peebles and Martin had requested assistance from the Pringles in the shifting of some of his ponderous equipment to the china closet where the *famille-rose* was stored. Minus one plate that Hope had thrown to the floor. Now that her enemy was so decisively removed, the rest was, presumably, safe. She must be as pleased as Faith that the obstacle was no longer there.

Abigail changed into her habit. It was neat and dark but not very bridal. Still, there were no hard-and-fast rules about what one must wear at a wedding. There were some white flowers she'd noticed outside the gate when she was brought back by Geoffrey from the Hanging Tower. She would take some of those. At the thought of Crichton awaiting her arrival a curious faintness possessed her. Only God knew if what she was doing made sense.

She took a last look in the mirror. Jeannie had helped her to wash her hair yesterday and it was soft and loose. She looked vulnerable. Men took advantage when one appeared insecure.

Abigail let herself out of the room. The house was filled with creaks and whispers, quiet footfalls, occasional light running steps that would be the maids. Pringles may not be dainty but they were remarkably nimble. Glancing along the landing below, she saw a small maidservant at Peter's door. The girl was less masculine than the preponderance of Pringle females, and neater than most. But there was no time to see if the child gained admittance. She had an important appointment at Cauldshiel. Her heart gave a disconcerting flutter at the thought of the enormity of the occasion.

Two men were removing photographic equipment from the stable when she went to saddle Suzy. Martin stepped out just as she hurried into the stall where the mare whickered in recognition.

'Enjoy yourself.'

'I intend to,' she answered curtly.

'There were reasons,' he said, 'why I had to refuse. Believe me –'

'Do not apologize.' Her fingers were unsteady on the girths.

'I am no more a free agent than you.'

'No?'

'Oh, well. If you are determined on obstinacy!'

'Not at all. I am no longer interested.'

'But you'll do nothing irrevocably foolish on the rebound?'

Abigail yawned ostentatiously. 'Do you mind? I wish to go and you are blocking my way.'

Martin muttered something under his breath and shifted to one side.

'Thank you, Mr. Martin.' She did not look back, the temporary triumph swiftly overlaid with a chill little patina of misery. All the way down the drive she was conscious of being seen from the trees, of the mounted Pringles, now on the long whaleback ridge behind the house. They straggled briefly on the edge of vision then were gone behind the bouncing foliage.

She wished she had not seen Martin, that she had listened to his explanation, relieved she was not stopped at the gate. The Inspector had obviously sent a message directly after breakfast. The white flowers, which had either been planted by the lodgekeeper or had seeded themselves, were fresh and dainty. She had provided herself with cotton and pins so was able to make them into a neat spray to pin on to her jacket, then continued on her way past the pale pink wall.

The weather was a little boisterous, which was common to the region, and the breeze soon brought the colour to her normally pale face and brightened her eyes to a sharp green. Tendrils of hair brushed her lips and cheeks. The tower drowned her in shadow as she forded the stream. She bit back a cry as a figure detached itself from the back of the building. It was Crichton in his elegant grey coat and high cravat, his curls subdued by a tall hat that gave him the look of a stranger, leading a horse by the rein.

'I feared you would not come.'

'I promised.'

'Was there no difficulty?'

'Remarkably little. Suspiciously little, I thought.'

He smiled. 'I cannot say how pleased I am to see you.'

His hands looked the same, she thought, tough and brown. How would they feel on naked flesh? Her stomach muscles contracted.

'The flowers. Did they not arouse curiosity?'

'I picked them from the hedge outside.'

He swung himself astride and leaned towards her. 'I suppose I am allowed to kiss you now?'

She wished there had not been that shadow from the tower, or that his coat was not grey. For days she had not thought of the gipsy but now all the foreboding rushed to overwhelm her anew. Nothing about their plans seemed right.

'I – suppose you are.'

She turned her face and felt his lips, strong and warm against her mouth.

EIGHT

'You said an hour or two,' Martin said as Abigail emerged from the stall after returning Suzy.

'I did come back.' She dragged her mind away with an effort from wine and kisses.

'You do not seem pleased about it.'

'It is a temporary return. I – I have somewhere else to go, only I needed my clothes and belongings.'

'That does sound decisive,' he remarked, frowning. 'But you know what the Inspector said.'

'He cannot keep me here for ever just because I was the first to discover Mrs Rutherford's body and her son thought I behaved suspiciously.'

'But he can order you to stay until her body has been found and examined for a cause of death.'

'I wish to leave as soon as possible.'

'May one ask why?'

'Because I have something better to do. Much better.' She was glad she had remembered to leave the flowers behind. They were in a glass of water on the wide, shabby windowsill of Cauldshiel.

'Be back,' Crichton had said, 'before they begin to fade.'

Abigail went slowly towards the stable door. The last hours had wrought havoc with her emotions. It had been hard not to break her promise to Scott and being faced with Martin now that she had burned her boats was doubly difficult.

Martin fell into step beside her. 'It will be supper in an hour or so. May we talk?'

'There is nothing now to discuss.'

'I see. Miss Menory, who do you think was responsible for Mrs Rutherford's death and disappearance? You must have your own ideas.'

'I hardly like to say. Any suggestion must malign someone.'

'But you've obviously given the matter thought.'

'Who has not?' Her riding boots crunched on the gravel that skirted the flagstoned porch.

'I have not forgotten Scott's violent reaction to Mrs Rutherford's suggestions. Or that Miss Hope almost certainly overheard them. Nor that Mrs Ward resented her supplanter or that young Mr Geoffrey could have feared a child of the projected marriage. Neither would Mr Crichton nor Miss Charity have cared for that prospect. And the Pringles detested every hair of her little, determined head, to a man –'

'And a woman.'

'I see you have not lost your sense of humour, Miss Abigail, whatever else you may have forfeited today.'

'You think – I am in some way, deprived?'

'I cannot help my thoughts, remembering our earlier conversation. And I suspect you found a certain person, personable –'

'Conjecture, Mr Martin.'

'Returning to our mystery –'

'The Inspector's mystery.'

'Well, then?' The wide, shadowy hall engulfed them.

Abigail lowered her voice. 'I think there is a way out of the Peacock Room. And I have not forgotten that Giles Scott would have known of it, Felicity's husband. If he had gone to France, remarried, the children of the new marriage could have been let into the secret.'

'And waited for more than a century to use it? Why?'

'Perhaps there *have* been approaches over the years. And then, there is the matter of your dark room to which all are denied access.'

'Miss Menory! Do you accuse me?' He feigned dismay or she imagined he did.

'You asked me what I thought.'

'And I am beginning to doubt the wisdom of inviting comment. Incidentally, you know that the Inspector will expect an account of your doings today?'

'Oh?'

'I'm sorry if it is going to lead to awkwardness.' She could hardly see him in the dimness but his voice gave him away.

'I will tell him only what I think fit.'

'It may not be so easy,' he warned. 'Considering you were so long gone and no one seeing you after you made your posy. What have you done with it?'

'I shall be glad to be gone from here! It is a fortress of intrigue!' she protested.

'I should have known you'd find the apposite description. I will see you at supper.'

'I'm not hungry. I have eaten already.'

'And well, I'll be bound?'

'Well enough.' It had been more than well. There had been a duck from the pond, pigeons from the wood, trout from the stream. And enough wine to forget the gipsy with the basket of pegs and the colour of Crichton's coat. Enough to forget betrayal –

She moved her hand and saw the flash of the new ring, disturbing her afresh.

'You were not wearing that before,' Martin said sharply. 'I should have noticed.'

'No. I do not usually wear jewellery.'

'You did not have it on when you left.'
'No?'
'You know quite well you didn't! I hate pretence.'
'Excuse me. I wish to tidy myself.'

Martin's hand shot out and closed over her forearm. She was propelled, protesting, to the light. The ring winked on her finger, narrow, studded with a small green stone. 'God's teeth! I thought you joked. About having something better to do.'

'Let me go.' She kicked out at his shin and almost fell as he released her.

'A veritable Katherine,' he said bitterly as she hurried to the stair. 'I always thought there was a touch of the shrew in you.'

'Then you will not be disappointed.'

'But, Abigail –'

She continued to almost run up the steps.

'It's only glass!' Martin shouted after her. 'It's no emerald.'

'I know. I do not care.' She brushed past Faith who had appeared from nowhere, and continued upwards to the top floor. The Green Room was a cool, inviting sanctuary. Flinging herself on to the bed, she closed her eyes, remembering the piper who had played this afternoon at Cauldshiel, the white flowers in the glass, the wine in the chipped goblet, the old, sick man who was Crichton's father and had risen from bed to attend his son's wedding. The house and its environs had been thick with Youngs. She should not have done it. She knew it now.

Hamlet and Ophelia screamed loudly as Abigail went down to the dining-room. The sound was magnified by the height of the ceilings and old window-frames never fitted properly. Her hand tightened on the mahogany rail. The screams continued. One could commit murder and it would pass unnoticed, she reflected, then remembered the gipsy. Royal birds. She had mentioned them with the colour grey, shadows and something else Abigail could not remember. They were all part of this macabre situation.

She had, at first, decided to ignore supper but that would only have meant that she would be sought out in the Green Room. And the wedding breakfast had been a long time ago. Food would not be unwelcome even if her hunger was brought on by nervousness.

The green skirts swished over the inlaid floor. Her hand went up to her hair which was soft and curling after the steam of the bath. Green gown, green eyes and a green stone in the new ring. If only her hair were not so red —

There was only one vacant place at the table, her own. Peter Rutherford was there, looking pale but clean shaven, though his hand must have shaken as he did so, resulting in a red graze by his mouth. Hope looked pleased by his presence and had taken some trouble with her appearance.

Running the gauntlet of their concerted stares, Abigail took her seat next to Martin. Faith Ward's face looked even more like a doll's. Sir Humphrey appeared to have reverted to his more intimidating self. Accepting soup from the imperturbable Hod, Scott asked, 'Did you enjoy your visit to Cauldshiel today, Miss Menory?'

They said attack was the best form of defence and Scott had not been a soldier for nothing. Quite calmly, Abigail replied, 'I enjoyed it very much,' and drank a spoonful of Scotch broth with perfect self-possession. She did not intend to amplify the statement.

'Why did you go there?' Scot pursued.

'I have received an invitation to stay with the Crichtons. I should like to avail myself of the proposal. Not that I am ungrateful, far from it, but I came to Duncraw to please someone who is no longer here. And I thank you, sincerely, for the hospitality I have received.' She hoped it did not sound too much like an afterthought.

'I'm sorry you should prefer the Crichtons to ourselves,' Sir Humphrey said stiffly, 'but as soon as the Inspector agrees, by all means go where you will.'

'Perhaps, in a few days,' the Inspector told Abigail, 'you may leave.'

'A few days!'

'My dear young miss, you must understand nothing if you imagine witnesses can wander off in the middle of an investigation,' he said with uncharacteristic firmness. 'You disappeared for hours yesterday and for all I knew might never come back.'

'But it is plain you all knew where I was. And I gave my word – I was merely – delayed.'

'I do not intend to quibble over the matter,' Inspector Moray told her. 'When my enquiry is complete, then, as Sir Humphrey says, you are free to go to Timbuctoo if you will –'

'I expressed no desire to go to Timbuctoo,' Abigail said rebelliously.

'You are being tiresome,' Martin said softly.

'Mind your own business.'

'The Inspector is right and I suspect that, under all that defiance, you know it.'

'I do not really want your opinion,' Abigail said.

'May I retrieve the photograph I gave you?'

'Of course.' For some reason she hated to agree. The picture was something she would have preferred to keep, to frame, to cushion the buffets of growing old.

'Only until I make a copy.'

'Oh. I'm glad you did not want to take it permanently.'

'Then, I have succeeded in doing something right?'

'Very right. There was one thing I noticed, a kind of blemish – very tiny.'

'A blemish?'

'I wondered if it could be removed from the second photograph. Something adhering to the plate, perhaps?'

'Things do not usually adhere to my plates,' he said indignantly, and Abigail found herself laughing.

'Then I can come for the photograph?'

'Come for it?'

'I have not provided it with legs.' How waspish he could be!

'I think it would be better if we met on neutral territory. The withdrawing-room?'

'Very well. In half an hour?'

Her bed-chamber enclosed her in its particular brand of sea-green shade. Jeannie had lit a small fire of apple-logs which smelt smokily fragrant and Abigail would have been happy to stay there, but if she did that, then Martin would come knocking at the door and she wanted no private confrontation with him.

All the way down to the withdrawing-room, she thought of what she and Martin would say to one another. The geranium red curtains and small stuffed chair contrasted so well with the general whiteness of the room. The bright cushions on the big ivory-covered sofa and the little white chair that Charity had always preferred were a warm mixture of pink and vermilion. Where was Charity at this moment?

Martin's entry filled her with relief. Let her get this meeting over as quickly as possible, then escape.

He took the photograph, then sat down in the red chair and produced a large magnifying glass from one pocket of his stylish coat. Abigail remained standing in an effort to impress upon him the transience of her presence. Leaning over the picture, she pointed to the small round darkness that marred the background. 'It's very small. Hardly worth mentioning – '

'Not at all.' He stared at it so fixedly through the glass that she was driven to ask if she might look. Martin handed her the magnifier and waited. It was astonishing, Abigail thought, how enormous everything appeared.

The carving of the peacock sprang out at her, so solid that she could have touched it. The folds of the hangings seemed to sway. Her memory stirred uncomfortably.

The dark circle she had noticed emerged from the intricate woodwork, not very large but perfectly round. She had an impression of darkness beyond darkness as though of another dimension. 'It's – very regular. Almost like – ' She stopped, unwilling to commit herself.

'Like a spy-hole?' Martin suggested almost idly. 'It's like a peep-hole, isn't it?'

Her tongue felt, suddenly, too large for her mouth. 'Like that. But why did you not notice it yourself?'

'Because I was looking at you. I couldn't see anything else. Careless of me.'

She swallowed. 'What will you do?'

'What will I do? Ask Sir Humphrey to open up that wretched room. That's what.'

The Inspector had been shown the magnified peep-hole, if that was what it was, and Sir Humphrey was summoned, reluctantly, from his study. Abigail was rigid with excitement. She had not been asked to leave the withdrawing-room and, indeed, would have refused since she had been first to see the tiny blemish she had taken for a spot of dirt on the plate.

Hod Pringle had come with Scott, waiting impassively by the window, his grey head outlined against the dusk.

One of the peacocks screamed and Hod's head turned on the instant to stare from the window.

'Damn those birds!' Sir Humphrey said ill-humouredly.

'I'll see to them, shall I?' Hod offered. 'Time they were penned in.'

'If you will. Then come back.'

'Here?'

'No. To the Peacock Room.'

A curious glance passed between them.

'Very well.' Hod went.

'I confess I had not noticed the spot,' Martin was saying while the Inspector stared disapprovingly over his shoulder. 'Miss Menory, who has extremely good sight, she informs me, noticed the regularity of the small imperfection. I had to use the magnifying glass to see it. There. Look for yourselves.'

First the Inspector, then Scott, made their own painstaking examination.

'So you see, Sir Humphrey, we should investigate the room further. Who keeps the keys?'

'I have one. Hod has another he shares with Mrs Davison.'

'Have you the key with you?' the Inspector asked.

'Yes.'

'Then I propose we go there, taking this photograph.'

'As you wish.'

The three men left the room. Abigail followed. The door of Peter Rutherford's bed-chamber stood ajar, emitting a pale flood of light. From the servants' stair, the voice of Mrs Davison rose sharply.

Hamlet and Ophelia had stopped their raucous pleasantries. Scott opened the door of the Peacock

Room in an uncanny silence and went to light candles. The ceiling bounced with shadows. Martin took another look at the photograph. 'The spot is just above – let me see - the stem of the rose that projects beyond the edge of the tail to the right of the bed. Beside the trailing branch. Where the rose and the branch almost meet.'

The Inspector was hopping about on one of the chairs, regardless of his feet on the green cushion, his stubby fingers feeling the ridges of the panelling. 'There is a small, round indentation. Quite shallow. Do you think this has just caught the shadow?'

'But why is it there?' Martin asked. 'In exactly the same spot the camera had shown what appears to be a hole, you find a shallow depression. A woman has vanished from the bed. It seems too great a coincidence. What do you think, Sir Humphrey?'

For what seemed an age, Scott stood still and pale. Then he shrugged. 'I should have told you sooner.'

'Told what?' the Inspector enquired, stopping his trampling of the green velvet. Abigail held her breath.

'That there is a passage.'

'Then why – ?'

'It is not the kind of thing one broadcasts. If everyone knows, advantage can be taken. And you know of recent problems. I need not go further into those. It did not seem necessary at first since my secret was shared by one only. One I could trust implicitly. But when Miss Menory made her discovery, then Eleanor disappeared, I knew that I should be suspect. That quarrel had obviously been overheard, and when Hope's name was dragged into the affair, I feared for her – in case she had discovered what I already knew. Hope – moves quietly. Is often where one does not expect her to be. And she enjoyed surprising me. I could not be quite sure that she had not, at one time, seen the wall open. Since one would need to be blind and deaf to be unaware of her antipathy for Eleanor, I kept silent.'

'And,' the Inspector said softly, 'the – other?'

'Other?'

'The one who knew. Besides yourself.'

'Must I say?'

'Really, Sir Humphrey,' the Inspector insisted in a very different tone. 'You know you must. Not that we cannot hazard a guess.'

'You'd best tell them,' Hod said woodenly, back from fastening up the birds for the night. 'Or, better still, I'll tell them. I knew. Only the master and myself, just as it used to be Sir John and my father.'

'The passage was built into the house at the beginning. It had its uses – '

'The Crichtons must have known at the start,' Martin suggested, stroking the edges of the photograph. 'They'd not allow enemies into the valley. They'd be allies at first. We can be reasonably sure of that. Perhaps they still know and even if the secret had been forgotten, they might have been reminded. You have another daughter.'

'I had another daughter.'

'She still exists,' Abigail muttered, then subsided.

'I should have thought you'd have done better to keep quiet on that subject,' Martin said very quietly.

'Have you used the passage since Mrs Rutherford's disappearance?' the Inspector was asking. 'Either of you?'

'I took Hod with me after the search had moved downstairs. But there was nothing.'

'I think we should look again.'

'Hod. Would you fetch the lantern?'

The man nodded and went as quietly as he had come. No one seemed inclined to speak. Kenith Martin twiddled the picture of Abigail and the Inspector turned his attention to the carving while he whistled tunelessly between his teeth.

Sir Humphrey pulled himself together with Hod's return. 'Close the door. What excuse did you give for the lantern?'

'Said I was going to look for a rat.'

Scott moved past Moray towards the wall. His fingers moved over the protuberances of part of the peacock's tail below the rose that marked the small concavity the Inspector had detected. There was a soft, grinding noise and a portion of the wooden wall tilted to disclose a narrow opening. Abigail moved towards the gap as though hypnotized.

'Then the story of Felicity Croser was true?' Martin was saying, staring into the obscurity.

'Yes. There's no doubt that she was – visited once she was asleep. Probably smothered, then taken out and put in the river.' Scott sounded almost matter-of-fact.

Abigail remembered what it was the gipsy had warned her about. Water. Greyness, shadows, water and royal birds. She had forgotten the water. How terrible to be seventeen and caught up in a feud between opposing families. Like being Juliet, doomed before her life had really begun.

'Then the Crichtons must have known at that time of the existence of the entrance to the room. Logically, it could have been no one else,' Martin said.

'We can never know for certain,' Scott admitted. 'Oh, come if you are coming, Miss Menory! It would be useless to deny you with one foot over the threshold. You remind me of – Eleanor.' His voice died away.

Abigail lifted her green skirts and stepped into the lamplit cavity. She turned just as Sir Humphrey pressed a lever set into the stone and had a glimpse of the Peacock Room from this strange angle. She thought ridiculously that the door was open a little but before she could be certain the panel had begun to move back then fell into place with a click.

The flap of the spy-hole was plainly visible from this side. Abigail toyed with the notion of opening it but was almost afraid of what she might see. And she would not want to be left behind.

Looking around her, the dust pricking at her nose, she saw a small stone recess from which steps led downwards. Scott had followed Hod who carried the lantern which swung, sending shadows scudding up the wall like clouds. His thick blond hair dipped and was gone. The Inspector went next.

'Take care you do not trip over your skirts,' Martin said. 'If you fall, you fall on me.'

'Oh. I thought for a moment you were being solicitous.'

'You would not be Abigail without that tiny touch of acid.'

'It need not trouble you for long. When she's found, I'll be able to go.'

'Back to Cauldshiel. Is that what you really want?'

'Yes. I am – committed.'

He was quiet then, taking his turn on the stair that turned and twisted in a shallow spiral. It would be difficult carrying a body down here. She experienced a moment of repugnance. Voices ascended, low and echoing, then Martin stumbled on to level flagstones and she saw a longish, narrow passage that ended at a high wall.

Hod released the mechanism and the wall was split with narrow blackness. She knew where they were because of the marble statue that confronted them. She had seen it standing in a concave niche. The sort of niche one would take for granted since it was balanced by another looking exactly the same at the other end of the terrace. Shrubs gave cover to anyone approaching the alcove.

'There's no body, then,' the Inspector said in tones of disappointment. Abigail caught sight of his sandy hair, wild and tousled in the lantern light.

'Of course there's a body,' Martin asserted, almost filling the gap. 'But it's been taken away. Put somewhere else – '

'I know where it is,' Abigail heard herself say. 'It's in the well. The old well. He tried to say it was a sheep's skull – '

'Who did?'

'Hod. Hod Pringle.'

They had been gone for some time with ropes, lanterns and heavy boots.

Peter, alerted by the footsteps and voices, had come downstairs and insisted upon accompanying the search party.

'Are you sure?' the Inspector asked.

'Of course, I'm sure. She is my mother.'

'You have been unwell. It could upset you – '

'I have spent years in a training meant to ensure that I can cope with anything.'

'But a stranger would mean much less, surely?'

'All human life has the same value.' There was a raw note of anger in Peter's voice that carried its own conviction. 'Anyone who takes it is beyond the pale.' Something in his pallor and resolution was disturbing. Peter would be a force to be reckoned with if Eleanor's murderer were ever named.

It was quiet after they left. Abigail drank tea and set herself to read diligently while she awaited the return of the search party. But the words began to dance in front of her eyes and she thought longingly of the Green Room and the probably already sleeping form of Jeannie who had decided to retire first since she was due to rise at five a.m. If she had the girl in her own household, Abigail decided, she would never want any human creature to get up at such an unearthly hour. Seven o'clock would be the earliest she'd expect service and that only in summer. Who really cared if one could see one's face in the surround of the stove? Life was for making the most of one's senses – talents.

They were coming back from the well. She could hear the ring of boots on the flags, the mutter of voices. Like reivers coming back from a raid. It must have sounded so two hundred years ago. Three. Crichtons and Scotts returning together, laughing, triumphant. Then came the hanging at the tower, the killing of a seventeen-year-old girl in reprisal. Now, the murder of Scott's woman? She could not believe it of Crichton. The echoes of his voice returned, 'Come back before the flowers fade.' Only she no longer knew if she could.

The door of the room opened and she saw a haze of silhouetted figures around the central, dishevelled presence of Martin who lurched forward mumbling, 'Alas poor Yorick,' and fell face forward on to the carpet, his hand disgorging something white and shining that rolled towards her.

Trust him to do something flamboyant, she thought ages later when Martin was put to bed with hot bricks and a bandage round his bombastic head. It was he, who, being a climber of some repute – what was he not? – had volunteered to descend into the bowels of the well. Some of the coping had loosened with the friction of the rope and a couple of stones had fallen on him, temporarily stunning him. A loss of blood had caused him to become faint when he reached the house and to release the sheep's skull that bore out the truth of Hod's testimony.

Kneeling by Martin's unconscious body, she had apologized to Hod and to the entire party who had gone on a wild-goose chase of her making. But the Inspector had said she behaved quite correctly. No one could accept the story of one person without proof and that proof was only to be found at the well's bottom. But Scott's face was stormy and he'd reproached her for having been the cause of Martin's injury.

'You might have deprived him of his ability to work. Or even of his life,' he added.

'I'm sorry. I thought –'

'Women think too much,' he broke in. 'Some women –'

'I think we should not judge her too hardly,' the Inspector pronounced pacifically. 'In fact, it is to Miss Menory's credit that she has sought so assiduously for –' then catching Peter's eye, he ended, 'what we have all tried to find.'

'And are there other places you would like investigated?' Scott asked Abigail sarcastically. 'Or are you now satisfied?'

'There were the old mine workings,' she said, stung. 'And the room under the Hanging Tower.'

'The tower is none of my business. And the mine workings are waterlogged.'

'I was right about the Peacock Room.'

'And sadly wrong about the well,' Sir Humphrey snapped. His eyes were very blue, she noticed, and much of his hang-dog air had dissipated.

'I have said I am sorry for that.'

The Inspector interrupted, 'The ponds will be dragged tomorrow.'

Then Martin had groaned and opened his black, Stuart eyes, seeing Abigail's anxious face looking down at him.

'Am I – dreaming?'

'A stone fell on your head. It was my fault. Are you all right?'

'A stone? Oh, yes. The well. I seem to recall bringing you a trophy.'

'It's over there, on the carpet. Could someone be sent for hot water and clean linen?' Abigail asked Scott.

He jerked across the room and tugged at the bell-pull, then told Molly, who appeared, her eyes red-rimmed, obviously from Mrs Davison's haranguing, to fetch what Miss Menory needed. The sheep's skull, which had settled in an upright position, seemed to watch the entire proceedings from its shadowy resting-place.

'Could it be removed?' Abigail asked as she finished fastening the linen strip securely. 'It is enough that I am accused by human eyes. I find that to be glared at by a sheep is *too* unnerving.'

Martin laughed as she thought he would, and his amusement lightened her load of guilt. The great well saga had become a farce and she disliked feeling foolish as well as responsible for his injuries.

Hod picked up the skull and carried it from the room with perfect Shakespearean panache. Abigail saw Martin grin and could not restrain a smile. Then he was assisted to his bedchamber by Scott and the Inspector, and, the fire being almost out, Abigail was forced to go to the Green Room where Jeannie lay, already asleep after her tiring day, and perform her toilette by the light of one small candle and a maximum of caution so that the girl was not awakened.

As soon as she was in bed, she pinched out the flame and lay staring into the dimness. She was not sure when she first noticed the noise or even what it was she heard – and then there was a familiarity about the sound, a soft grating or grinding that died out to leave a greater silence in its wake.

Jeannie stirred and turned over. 'Miss? What was that noise?'

'Noise? Sir Humphrey says noise carries up here from below,' Abigail said.

'It was like – something being dragged.'

'Nothing was; I was awake! Some door being closed.' Abigail's ears strained to hear some further scrape or footfall.

'Miss! There it is again. A sort of dragging. Oh, dear God! It's in that room.'

Jeannie had leapt from the bed and was standing, her teeth chattering with fright.

'It's all right,' Abigail told her gently. 'Everyone you could mention has been in the Peacock Room this evening – or yesterday might be more appropriate.'

'That's what I mean! It's too late for any ordinary soul – '

'I should have thought so.' Abigail had risen and was putting on her house-robe, fastening the belt with unsteady fingers. She picked up the candle-stick, ready to go out into the passageway.

'Don't leave me, miss! It's *her*. I know it is, come back – '

'Come with me, there's nothing to fear. Bring the poker if you like.'

Jeannie, trembling, did as she was told. Cautiously, Abigail opened the door and went outside, the maid close behind her. She was just in time to see a grey figure vanish down the servants' stair. Abigail prepared herself to follow but Jeannie gave a moan and fell slowly to the floor, her face the colour of tallow.

Abandoning all thoughts of a chase, Abigail knelt down beside her.

NINE

Breakfast was late. Peter Rutherford had been roused by Abigail's efforts to lift Jeannie back on to the camp-bed and he had gone for Sir Humphrey who had listened to Abigail's story with a weary scepticism. Hod, never far from his master, had arrived in the middle of the recounting and it was only minutes later that the Inspector joined them, wearing a house-robe Abigail could only describe as loud. She half-expected Martin but the Inspector said the photographer was sleeping like the dead after a nightcap intended to dull the ache in his head.

The servants' stair was searched and also the kitchens and any passage that ran off from that portion of the house, plus the rooms that were on those floors, but there was no sign of an intruder. The only discovery of any interest was that a back door was found unbolted.

Scott was inclined to dismiss the grey apparition as fancy. 'I think we may conclude that the vision was a figment of Miss Menory's invention – not deliberate,' he supplemented, seeing Abigail's expression, 'but nevertheless, a fantasy.'

'The earlier happenings – ' she began incautiously.

'Are a closed book, remember?' the Inspector reminded warningly.

'Of course. I'm sorry. It would be much simpler if

you were to agree to my going to Cauldshiel tomorrow. It seems I am disrupting the household.'

'I see no reason why you should not,' the Inspector replied. 'But you would not leave the Crichtons without informing me, would you, Miss Menory?'

Martin joined them at last, his dark face a little grey and tired but registering definite anger and disappointment when Abigail said, 'Sir Humphrey, may I beg one favour?'

'And what is that?' Scott asked without enthusiasm.

'May I borrow Suzy to ride to Cauldshiel? And, if my baggage could be sent later, I'll have her returned with the carriage? Or the trap, as the case may be.'

'I suppose so,' Scott answered distantly.

'So, you are leaving,' Martin said quietly.

'You knew I intended to.'

'Shall I not see you again?' The sad, dark eyes reproached her.

'I think not. What was your wife's name, Mr. Martin?'

'Elspeth.'

'Oh. She was – fair, I suppose?' She could not go without satisfying her curiosity.

'And why should you suppose that? No. She was rather like you, much the same colouring and general appearance.'

'Would you make the same mistake twice?' Abigail could not forbear to ask.

'There is no danger of that now.' His face closed up. He looked weary and a good deal older than on the day of his magnificent arrival. The bandage emphasized the thick blackness of his hair and the brown of his skin. Abigail was conscious, stupidly, of a compulsion to protect him as she had always done with Charity.

* * *

Abigail did not wish to go to Cauldshiel via the drive and the pink wall, so she turned Suzy's head in the opposite direction and took the route she and Charity had chosen on her second day at Duncraw. The hill, patched with sunlight and shade, had a pleasant familiarity, the upper slopes planted with part firs, part deciduous trees. Opening a small gate in the wall, she bent to latch it after her and set off slowly over the heathery moor that spread as far as the woods. There was still some mist in the valley and this hazed the house and gardens with a mysterious bloom, drifting through the massed shrubs like incipient fires.

The graveyard with its tiny chapel flaunted its small plantation of crosses in a hushed silence. Sheep nibbled as far as the entrance, hardly bothering to raise their heads from the still-damp grass. There lay the victims of pestilence, of wars that were almost forgotten, of extreme youth and of old age. And there too lay Johanne, her bones all crushed, and the remains of Felicity Croser, dead of a vendetta.

A bird flew up out of the cemetery and was quickly followed by another. Tracing the line of their unexpected flight, Abigail saw a small figure in the distance. She had little but an impression of a white horse and a grey cloak. The rider picked its anonymous way carefully, skirting the edge of the trees that came down much lower as one progressed round the hill's flank to overlook the no-man's-land between the two houses.

The white horse reminded Abigail of the one Charity always used and something about the figure struck her as being more feminine than masculine, though, from this distance, she could not decide what gave her the impression. Had Charity been driven by some unexpected nostalgia to take a look at her former home?

The sheep trail widened into a decisive track that

edged the perimeter of the woods and Abigail began to ride a little faster, not wanting to call out to Charity unless she were perfectly certain it was Scott's daughter. Underneath Charity's bitterness, Abigail thought she had detected a longing to be loved by him and this visit seemed to bear out the truth of the theory. She could see the untidy mounds of the opencast coal site now, not very extensive, the hummocks weed-grown with gleaming pools in the hollows between. The ponds were dark and a few gulls clustered round them, rising into the air in strong white arcs as the Pringles began to advance across the short distance remaining. Abigail made out the figure of Scott, outstanding because of his thick, pale hair, and the Inspector. Hod, as always, was close to Scott, his fowling-piece carried in the military fashion old soldiers never lose. Martin seemed not yet to be there.

The figure on the white horse had vanished. Puzzled, Abigail could not see how she could have lost the rider so completely. A group of Pringles were prodding the first pool with long sticks. One gave a shout and the entire party converged on it, shouting and gesticulating. Hod took the stick from his henchman and thrust it deftly into the middle of the dark pond where it seemed to stick on something more solid than mud.

She tried to beat down the incipient sickness. Three men waded out, their feet encountering the obstacle which Hod had struck. They bent, arms and chests disappearing into three feet of water, tugging and hoisting until the dark, sodden thing they had rescued was plain to view. It was about the size of a human torso, Abigail saw, then turned away to lean against the nearest tree-trunk. Someone called out, then there was an uneasy silence followed by a subdued murmur of voices. It had to be Eleanor, she realized. They had looked everywhere else.

Averting her face, she began to ride in the direction of Cauldshiel. Her black habit and the equally dark hide of the mare merged into the shadow of the trees. No one below was likely to see her act of cowardice. She still could not make out the figure of Martin, or even any trace of white bandage, but the scene was congested and far away.

Abigail stopped suddenly, hearing a crashing in the trees some way ahead. The rider, it appeared, was returning. She waited, listening to the cracking of sticks and the swish of branches, half her attention on the mine area where everyone just stood, waiting for fresh orders and murmuring together, and the other suddenly conscious that the sounds from the wood had stopped. A tall pine protruded from the green froth of larch that half-surrounded Cauldshiel, the topmost branches dead and white as though killed by lightning. Beyond the bone-bareness of this tree, the Crichton house crouched in a clearing, bleakly grey, showing from this unaccustomed angle, three small steeples of varying sizes. Here, in this part of the country, she always felt this sense of timelessness. The fugitive sunlight, the thinning mist in the lowermost reaches of the valley, the colours of the day all served to accentuate the mingled terror and permanence of her surroundings.

Pressing herself closer under the gigantic shade of a chestnut tree that overhung the track, Abigail waited. Her heart thumped suddenly as the head and forelegs of the white horse appeared from the thinning fringe of brush and bracken that marked the wood's ending. A booted foot and a capable hand on the rein, an impression of greyness through the fine mesh of delicate branches. The same nameless rider –

A cold fear possessed her. The white horse moved forward a pace, dislodging a runnel of small pebbles.

A hand, smallish and feminine, she noted clinically while recoiling from the deep shadow that filled the hood of the cloak, hiding all trace of feature, rose to point in the direction of Sir Humphrey's blond head. The hand held a pistol of some kind. Too large a weapon for a woman, Abigail thought, then exploded into a flurry of activity, goading forward the reluctant mare, crying out just as the weapon went off with a hideous bang.

'No, Charity! No – no – '

But it was too late. Scott staggered and swayed. The grey-cloaked figure turned to stare from the obscurity of that disguising hood showing a portion of rounded chin. 'What have you done?' Abigail whispered. 'Charity?'

The white horse leapt as the rider turned to flee up the trail through the trees. There was an answering percussion from the direction of the ponds and the grey-clad form jerked, groaned, flung up protesting arms and for a long moment was hideously still. It was Hod who had fired.

The woman slumped forward just as the white horse reared in fright, blood showing on its hide, then began to crash at a headlong pace through the roughnesses of the woodland ride. One leg jerked free so that the body was flung over the animal.

Shouts drifted up from the mine workings as Abigail twisted Suzy's head round to follow. The woman hung now by one stirrup, her body bouncing like a sack of flour, her head striking the stumps of cut trees, a hand and wrist protruding briefly from within the cloak's concealing folds, then swept out of sight under a pile of leaf mould that sent up pungent smells of past autumns.

Suzy made a protesting sound the white horse recognized for all its recent fright. It went more slowly then at a half-hearted trot to stop altogether, its body trembling. Abigail got down, her legs buckling, and staggered towards the beast, releasing the imprisoned foot. The figure sprawled on the beech-mast and tree roots, terribly still. Abigail knelt, hesitated, then pulled back the hood to look down on the disfigured face.

'Are you feeling better?' Charity asked.

Abigail sat up. Her mind still remembered horror and creeping dreams she had tried to hold at bay through the drug of sleep. 'I'm all right. What about your father?'

'Very ill, Dr Craig says. He lost a great deal of blood. I think he'll die.'

'Hod will never let him.'

'There are some things even Hod cannot do.'

'I don't even know why *she* did it. I was banished before the inquest.'

'You'd had enough for one day. If it had not been for you she'd have escaped. Another minute and she'd have been in the trees. Gone for good.'

'I did nothing. It was chance. She never looked back, you see, and even if she had I would most probably have merged in with the wood's shade. Does your father realize he's at Cauldshiel?'

'No.'

'Ironic, isn't it?'

'Very.'

'And even more so to see Hod consorting with Youngs.'

'He sits outside Father's door like some guard dog. I think they're afraid of him.'

'What does Colin think of it all?'

A surge of colour stained Charity's white face. Something in her eyes and the set of her mouth told Abigail she had not done the wrong thing in spite of misgivings.

'Why don't you ask me?' Crichton said from the shadows and moved forward to lay his hand on Charity's shoulder. She leaned against him with a sigh.

'What do you think?' Abigail asked Crichton, pulling the bedclothes higher.

Crichton bestowed on Abigail the look of amused irony with which he always favoured her. She recognized it now for no more than that.

'It seems Scott's past caught up with him.'

'Did you know that my father had already had two narrow escapes from death?' Charity asked, removing herself reluctantly from Crichton's proprietorial grasp to relapse into the bedside chair.

'No!' The coming dusk oppressed her.

'Apparently someone shot at Father on two previous occasions and he, of course, informed the police. They arranged to send some high official on the pretext that various articles had been stolen, only it was Hod who, on Father's instructions, took one object at a time over a period with Father concealing the things in his study. He noticed the jade had gone and thinking it was Hod's doing mentioned it to the Inspector. He'd forgotten the statuette was mine.'

'Shall we have our possessions photographed as a safeguard?' Crichton queried. They both laughed and moved towards one another. Abigail was silent.

'I suppose,' she said, 'that Mr Martin will no longer be needed now that everything is in the open?'

'No. He will not,' Charity murmured absently. 'I believe he is packing his paraphernalia at this moment and doubtless we will hear his juggernaut departure from as far away as Cauldshiel. It will be like the journey of the Trojan horse.'

Abigail, made unhappy by the news of Martin's departure, said, 'I will get up. Is it nearly supper time?'

'In half an hour.'

'I'm sorry the ring we gave you was not more valuable,' Charity remarked, seeing Abigail's white hand against the counterpane. 'But we had to thank you somehow for being my attendant. It should have been an emerald.'

'At least it will match my eyes,' Abigail replied. 'Remember? Green glass?'

Abigail dashed water over her face and tidied her hair. Why could she not have accepted Martin on his own terms while he was there? What was the point of being with principles and without the man for whom she had come to entertain an all-absorbing passion? But it was too late and the thought was arid.

Cauldshiel's shabby panelling was unimpressive but comfortingly cosy. She walked quietly into the room with the wide window seat and the battered cushions. The candles were not yet lit and only the pink fireglow lay over everything. She thought at first that she was alone, then saw that one chair drawn up to the hearth was occupied. Abigail stared at the high back that concealed all but one elbow, the one foot that swung idly.

'Inspector Moray?' she said in a voice that cracked foolishly.

'Yes.'

The Inspector seemed to be having the same difficulty since he replied in a near whisper.

'Charity said you would be here but it seems I've come down too soon for supper.'

'Not too soon.' The voice was a little louder now. And familiar – 'Not for me.'

'Do not play games! You are supposed to be at Duncraw. Packing – ' She was angry.

'But, I told you, I am the Inspector. Mr Martin *is* packing. I am Moray.'

'I don't understand.'

Martin – Moray had risen to face her, a black, Stuart outline against the fire.

'Why the masquerade?'

'Whoever threatened Scott would be far more interested in a policeman than in a photographer.'

'Then, is it the Inspector – I mean Mr Martin – who had a wife called Elspeth?'

There was a pause. 'No. It was I. It was not the perfect marriage. My hours are far from regular and that irritated Elspeth who liked things cut and dried. But don't think it was all a one-sided affair. I could not see that I should have been more understanding, and I have never enjoyed being – possessed. The root of the matter was that we could not really have loved one another. James was only two when she left me for another man –'

'With the child?'

'No. He reminded her too much of me, she said. She died later of a neglected chill.'

'I'm sorry.'

'What is there to be sorry for? I should apologize to you. Not all women can be bought with champagne and promises and to tell the truth I'm glad you refused me.'

Moray moved towards her and she could see him now, tall and dark, the mantle of careless amusement stripped away to leave a stranger. 'Abigail. I allowed myself to be deluded into believing that there was some satisfaction to be got from passing affairs. That they hurt no one. But it's not true, is it? I treated you badly and you deserve so much better. Tell me, are you like Elspeth? Would you rebel against a life that's unconventional? That could mean seeing me when it could be inconvenient and being without me during some domestic crisis. For, to tell the truth, I don't want to lose you too.'

Her voice had grown thick and cumbersome. Roughly, she burst out, 'It would *never* be inconvenient. How could it be?'

He had her in his arms and was kissing her so hard that the breath was knocked out of her body. 'I'm glad,' she said a little later, 'that your name isn't Martin. I never really thought it suited you. Not with that hint of Charles the Second.'

Charity and Crichton sat at either end of the table. Old Crichton, wrapped in a rug, sat opposite Abigail, his thin face tired but his eyes still keen and observant. He'd been very handsome once, in the same fashion as Colin. It was sad to see strength and physical beauty vanish. What a fool she'd have been to let Kenith Moray get away and both of them wasting their lives as a result. Her hand reached for his under shelter of the table.

'Abigail does not know the details of the affair,' Charity said. 'Could you enlighten her, Inspector?'

A detachment of square, sandy Youngs were beginning to serve at the frugal table. No fine linen, no candelabra here, only flowers in a glass jug, but the fire of logs was cheerful. Beyond the window, the purple bulk of Heartsease Hill filled the horizon.

'You were asleep when he finally told the story. The reasons for his mother's violent hatred and his part in the attempted murder.'

'We must go back to the Crimea for the motive. The war began in March of 1854, as you know, with Russia on one side and France and Britain on the other. The Crimea was invaded in September, the Russians defeated at Alma, then Balaclava. There was the dreadful business of the Light Brigade, doomed because of a mistake, and an elementary one at that, but we redeemed ourselves at Inkerman. The Russians retired to lick their wounds and we pressed on to Sebastopol. But it was winter by then and the weather and poor leadership took their toll. Well-trained men had to be replaced by immature recruits. Officers appeared who had no knowledge of the terrain and were ignorant of the conditions. Only the severest discipline kept the situation under control. Sir Humphrey was there, as you no doubt know already, Mrs Crichton – '

'Charity. Please call me that. Any friend of Abby's must also be ours.'

'As always, there was a no-man's-land, and it was impossible to tell exactly where the Russians were. It was a war of nerves and some nerves did not stand up to the strain. Sir Humphrey had in his detachment an officer called John Donaldson, a sensitive man, sickened by adverse conditions and the sight of dead soldiers. A Captain Grey who was in close contact with both Scott and Donaldson has told of how Sir Humphrey was totally unsympathetic to weakness, contemptuous of Donaldson for his foreseeable break-up, and took no trouble to conceal his disgust. Your father watched Donaldson closely, another factor in deciding Donaldson's eventual disintegration under a fire of grapeshot while they covered the French in an attempt to take the Malakoff Tower. He fled from the carnage, leaving his men to be shot to pieces. Scott accused him publicly of cowardice. Grey himself was badly wounded in the engagement and knew nothing of the outcome until he recovered from a fever brought on by his injuries to discover that Donaldson had already been shot. He could not forget the incident, and years later, when he met Donaldson's wife in Edinburgh and she was told that he too was at Sebastopol, he gave her his version of the execution. She had been told only that her husband had been killed during the engagement. The army had decided belatedly to be merciful. You can imagine the feelings of this woman and of her son, the bitterness of their resentment. They made it their business to discover Sir Humphrey's address and his habits and it did not take long to find out that his relations with the neighbouring Crichtons were not happy. They decided that they would take a life for a life, to try to break Sir Humphrey's nerve as Donaldson's had been broken. They maintained that had Scott withdrawn Donaldson, as he obviously should have done, and sent him to a hospital, that would have been proper and humane.

'They had no intentions of being caught after their act of vengeance, nor even of being suspected. Mrs Donaldson made an opportunity of meeting Sir Humphrey socially, under another name, of course, and being attractive, and Scott being lonely, she had herself invited to Duncraw — where the legend of the Peacock Bed gave her the idea of pretending to die there and thus to disappear like Felicity Croser. But, first of all, she had to arrange matters so that she antagonized as many of the inhabitants of the house as possible and particularly Scott, in order to divert attention from her accomplice, her son Peter.'

'How did you know Peter Rutherford was really called Donaldson?'

'We sent Bob Pringle to Edinburgh to contact the sergeant. He went to the Medical School and looked up the records. Peter had just graduated so he had to be on the last honours list. But there was no Rutherford listed, and fortunately, no other Peter but Donaldson. It would have been pointless to change his

Christian name and could even have been dangerous if his mother had made a slip of the tongue.'

'But I was convinced she was dead,' Abigail said. 'How could I be so wrong?'

'Peter is a good doctor for all his youth. He knew that a large dose of laudanum would give the appearance of death to almost anyone but to the Inspector, particularly if the flesh was cold. He knew that Abigail must hear the carefully engineered quarrel between his mother and Scott. He knew just how curious she would be and that she was an early riser, and that none of the servants would come upstairs unless summoned. The open door of the Peacock Room would be an irresistible magnet, allied with the open window that, because of the icy wind, was essential to make Eleanor Rutherford – Donaldson's body feel like that of a corpse. He knew to a hairsbreadth just how many drops of laudanum would be safe. And Abigail's testimony was essential.'

'But after that? The search?'

'That was the difficult part. He listened for you to run down to the study, and thinking he had only a few minutes – he was not to know Sir Humphrey was not, as usual at that time, in the study – he put Eleanor's body under your bed, Abigail. Then he went for the nightgown which was his alibi for supposedly leaving her alone on the Peacock Bed. Your delay in coming back must have rattled him as he must have realized he could have taken her to his own room in the time. Donaldson was going to pretend a breakdown as an excuse for shutting himself in. Matters took their inevitable progress. Scott and Abigail returned to the empty room but Abigail felt unwell and retired to her own bed-chamber, leaving Peter biting his fingernails, though that did him a good turn in that his room was searched with the others to disclose nothing.

'He waited in misery, for Eleanor needed treatment to recover, then when he went up to the Green Room on the pretext of questioning Abigail further, he found her in a deep sleep. He took Eleanor in a blanket and took her down to his own bed, and after that it was just a matter of pretending he was ill and asking for hot bricks to help revive his mother – giving her stimulants, keeping her out of sight until the moment of the attack on Sir Humphrey.

'Then,' Moray went on, 'Peter heard that the mine workings were to be searched. With every available person down in the valley and no horses nearby because of the waterlogged nature of the ground, Eleanor could fire her fatal shot – she was not a soldier's wife for nothing – and be over the hill and away long before she could be followed. With his mother's body never recovered – '

'What *was* that they took from the pond?' Abigail asked, shuddering.

'A sheep. They are accident-prone around Duncraw.'

'I think I still feel sorry for Peter, now that I've heard the whole story.' The purple hill cast a cold shadow. It would soon be dark.

'The last I saw of Hope,' Moray said, 'was being comforted by Geoffrey. She said something to the effect that she could no longer revere her father, that she could not entirely blame Peter and that a certain conversation she had had with Abigail had made her see that she must do something with her life. You must all do what you can, but I think Hope has changed, just in the nick of time. She must have a period of unhappiness, but at least she has emerged from that dangerous trauma over her mother's death.

There's a kindness in young Ward, and, after all, they've been together for years. It's familiarity she needs at present. Somebody sympathetic.'

'They took terrible chances,' Abigail said. 'Say someone had come upstairs at the wrong time?'

'No one knew about the Sebastopol affair. Peter would simply have said he'd made a mistake and that Eleanor had taken a sleeping draught – miscalculated the dose. And if she'd been found in his room, he would have said she had come to his door and had no memory of how she had come to be there. Another plan would have been hatched.'

'And that open spy-hole in the Peacock Room when you took my photograph?'

'Hod keeping a careful eye on the precious panelling because I had all that cumbersome equipment up there, while Scott was with the Inspector. The make-believe Inspector.'

'Why, that's his carriage now!' Charity cried.

The sound that Abigail had taken for a distant rumble of thunder was becoming accentuated. They got up from the table and rushed out on to the front steps, all but the old man who remained in his covering of plaid rug.

Down on the road, the four white shires pounded in unison. Carriage lamps glowed. The lowering sun caught at the tarnished gold on the purple lettering. Crichton shouted and the flap at the back of the carriage opened to reveal a bearded face, a mass of untidy, gingery hair.

'Goodbye! Goodbye!' the two girls cried, their arms around one another. Moray waved. The photographer waved back. Crichton laughed softly.

'Oh, dear,' Abigail said. 'I do think I might be going to cry. He was such a nice, little man.'

'I'm a nice, big man,' Moray said. 'Come, make use of my shoulder.'

So she did.

They went inside again eventually. A door was opened to reveal the pale-faced figure of Peter seated at a table upon which the remains of a meal lay disregarded. The sergeant beckoned to Moray.

Abigail's eyes met Peter's. She wanted to say something but no words came. The constable, large and watchful, hovered in the background. It was such a waste of a young life, she thought, agonized. But it was not a crime committed in the heat of the moment. There was something cold and unnatural in all that intense planning.

Moray came back to her and the door closed upon the desolate scene. He was used to this, Abigail realized, and she must accept his way of life, be there to distract him when his day's work was done. Help to take care of his child –

Crichton and Charity had returned to the supper table. Moray took Abigail's hand in a grip that hurt.

Someone came along the darkening passage. She thought at first that it was Crichton's father, old and frail, his footsteps dragging. But it was Hod Pringle, his shoulders bowed, his gaze seeing beyond them to a place where Scott still planned his tactics for the following day, where the bugle's note roused master and servant for the day's dangers or victories. Hod walked past them, opened the door and went out. A cold lick of air sent in a handful of leaves that twitched, found refuge in a doorway where they lay like mice.

'Hold me,' Abigail whispered. 'Hold me.'

Then the door closed with a final sound.

INTRODUCING...

Romantique

The Romance Magazine For The 1980's

Each exciting issue contains a full-length romance novel — the kind of first-love story we all dream about...

PLUS

other wonderful features such as a travelogue to the world's most romantic spots, advice about your romantic problems, a quiz to find the ideal mate for you and much, much more.

ROMANTIQUE: A complete novel of romance, plus a whole world of romantic features.

ROMANTIQUE: Wherever magazines are sold. Or write Romantique Magazine, Dept. C-1, 41 East 42nd Street, New York, N.Y. 10017

Romantique

INTERNATIONALLY DISTRIBUTED BY DELL DISTRIBUTING, INC.

Dell Bestsellers

- [ ] TO LOVE AGAIN by Danielle Steel $2.50 (18631-5)
- [ ] SECOND GENERATION by Howard Fast $2.75 (17892-4)
- [ ] EVERGREEN by Belva Plain $2.75 (13294-0)
- [ ] AMERICAN CAESAR by William Manchester . . . $3.50 (10413-0)
- [ ] THERE SHOULD HAVE BEEN CASTLES
  by Herman Raucher $2.75 (18500-9)
- [ ] THE FAR ARENA by Richard Ben Sapir $2.75 (12671-1)
- [ ] THE SAVIOR by Marvin Werlin and Mark Werlin . $2.75 (17748-0)
- [ ] SUMMER'S END by Danielle Steel $2.50 (18418-5)
- [ ] SHARKY'S MACHINE by William Diehl $2.50 (18292-1)
- [ ] DOWNRIVER by Peter Collier $2.75 (11830-1)
- [ ] CRY FOR THE STRANGERS by John Saul $2.50 (11869-7)
- [ ] BITTER EDEN by Sharon Salvato $2.75 (10771-7)
- [ ] WILD TIMES by Brian Garfield $2.50 (19457-1)
- [ ] 1407 BROADWAY by Joel Gross $2.50 (12819-6)
- [ ] A SPARROW FALLS by Wilbur Smith $2.75 (17707-3)
- [ ] FOR LOVE AND HONOR by Antonia Van-Loon . . $2.50 (12574-X)
- [ ] COLD IS THE SEA by Edward L. Beach $2.50 (11045-9)
- [ ] TROCADERO by Leslie Waller $2.50 (18613-7)
- [ ] THE BURNING LAND by Emma Drummond $2.50 (10274-X)
- [ ] HOUSE OF GOD by Samuel Shem, M.D. $2.50 (13371-8)
- [ ] SMALL TOWN by Sloan Wilson $2.50 (17474-0)

At your local bookstore or use this handy coupon for ordering:

Dell **DELL BOOKS**
P.O. BOX 1000, PINEBROOK, N.J. 07058

Please send me the books I have checked above. I am enclosing $_____
(please add 75¢ per copy to cover postage and handling). Send check or money order—no cash or C.O.D.'s. Please allow up to 8 weeks for shipment.

Mr/Mrs/Miss _____

Address _____

City _____ State/Zip _____

THE PASSING BELLS

by
PHILLIP ROCK

A story you'll wish would go on forever.

Here is the vivid story of the Grevilles, a titled British family, and their servants—men and women who knew their place, upstairs and down, until England went to war and the whole fabric of British society began to unravel and change.

"Well-written, exciting. Echoes of Hemingway, Graves and *Upstairs, Downstairs*."—*Library Journal*

"Every twenty-five years or so, we are blessed with a war novel, outstanding in that it depicts not only the history of a time but also its soul."—*West Coast Review of Books*.

"Vivid and enthralling."—*The Philadelphia Inquirer*

A Dell Book $2.75   (16837-6)

At your local bookstore or use this handy coupon for ordering:

| **Dell** | **DELL BOOKS**   THE PASSING BELLS $2.75   (16837-6)
P.O. BOX 1000, PINEBROOK, N.J. 07058 |

Please send me the above title. I am enclosing $_____
(please add 75¢ per copy to cover postage and handling). Send check or money order—no cash or C.O.D.'s. Please allow up to 8 weeks for shipment.

Mr/Mrs/Miss_____

Address_____

City_____State/Zip_____

Love—the way you want it!

Candlelight Romances

		TITLE NO.	
☐ THE CAPTIVE BRIDE by Lucy Phillips Stewart	$1.50	#232	(17768-5)
☐ FORBIDDEN YEARNINGS by Candice Arkham	$1.25	#235	(12736-X)
☐ HOLD ME FOREVER by Melissa Blakeley	$1.25	#231	(13488-9)
☐ THE HUNGRY HEART by Arlene Hale	$1.25	#226	(13798-5)
☐ LOVE'S UNTOLD SECRET by Betty Hale Hyatt	$1.25	#229	(14986-X)
☐ ONE LOVE FOREVER by Meredith Babeaux Brucker	$1.25	#234	(19302-8)
☐ PRECIOUS MOMENTS by Suzanne Roberts	$1.25	#236	(19621-3)
☐ THE RAVEN SISTERS by Dorothy Mack	$1.25	#221	(17255-1)
☐ THE SUBSTITUTE BRIDE by Dorothy Mack	$1.25	#225	(18375-8)
☐ TENDER LONGINGS by Barbara Lynn	$1.25	#230	(14001-3)
☐ UNEXPECTED HOLIDAY by Libby Mansfield	$1.50	#233	(19208-0)
☐ CAMERON'S LANDING by Anne Stuart	$1.25	#504	(10995-7)
☐ SUMMER MAGIC by F.C. Matranga	$1.25	#503	(17962-9)
☐ LEGEND OF LOVE by Louis Bergstrom	$1.25	#502	(15321-2)
☐ THE GOLDEN LURE by Jean Davidson	$1.25	#500	(12965-6)
☐ MOONLIGHT MIST by Laura London	$1.50	#263	(15464-4)
☐ THE SCANDALOUS SEASON by Nina Pykare	$1.50	#501	(18234-4)

At your local bookstore or use this handy coupon for ordering:

Dell | **DELL BOOKS**
P.O. BOX 1000, PINEBROOK, N.J. 07058

Please send me the books I have checked above. I am enclosing $ _____
(please add 75¢ per copy to cover postage and handling). Send check or money order—no cash or C.O.D.'s. Please allow up to 8 weeks for shipment.

Mr/Mrs/Miss _____

Address _____

City _____ State/Zip _____